PANHANDLE RAIDERS

OTHER TEXAS RANGER JIM BLAWCYZK NOVELS

By

JAMES J. GRIFFIN

TROUBLE RIDES THE TEXAS PACIFIC

BORDER RAIDERS

TRAIL OF THE RENEGADE

RANGER JUSTICE

AND COMING IN MID-2007 FROM CONDOR PUBLISHING, INC.

BIG BEND DEATH TRAP

A Texas Ranger Cody Havlicek Story

PANHANDLE RAIDERS

A Jim Blawcyzk Texas Ranger Story

James J. Griffin

For
Pete
Best
W. Shes!

iUniverse, Inc.
New York Lincoln Shanghai

PANHANDLE RAIDERS
A Jim Blawcyzk Texas Ranger Story

iUniverse books may be ordered through booksellers or by contacting:

iUniverse
2021 Pine Lake Road, Suite 100
Lincoln, NE 68512
www.iuniverse.com
1-800-Authors (1-800-288-4677)

ISBN: 978-0-595-44424-3 (pbk)
ISBN: 978-0-595-88752-1 (ebk)

Printed in the United States of America

Cover Illustration
Texas Rangers—Rimrock Sentinels
Original Painting—Acrylic on Canvas
By
Christopher Cofrancesco
Signed, Limited Edition Prints are available from the artist
Contact: efwchamp1@aol.com or (203)393-2111
Print Number One is in the permanent collection of the Texas Ranger
Hall of Fame and Museum in Waco, Texas

Author Photograph: Patricia Johnson
Digital Transfer Assistance: Ray O'Hara
Digital Enhancement: Gary Hennessey
Editorial Assistance: Kevin Smith

As always, the author wishes to thank Texas Ranger Sergeant Jim
Huggins of Company F, Waco, and Karl Rehn and Penny Riggs of KR
Training, Austin, Texas for their invaluable assistance on forensics and
weapons of the period, which helps keep my stories as accurate as possible within the realm of fiction.

For my nieces Jennifer, Rebecca, Victoria, and Samantha, and my nephews Jeffrey, Patrick, and Ronald.

CHAPTER 1

"It looks as if we're about to have company," Jeb Cummins worriedly remarked to his partner, Ace Corby, as their heavy Studebaker freight wagon jounced across the vast high plains of northwest Texas, carrying a load of goods bound from Abilene to the budding township of Lubbock. Both men had been studying the distant plume of dust marring the cloudless sky's deep azure for some time. The cloud had been steadily drawing nearer.

"That's quite a bunch of riders too, it seems like," Corby replied, turning his head and spitting to send a thick brown stream of tobacco juice spattering into the dust of the road. Some of the juice dribbled into his thick, matted beard. "I sure hope they don't aim to cause us any trouble. Those rifles we have for the Army post and some of the other stuff we're carryin' would make quite a haul for any hombres bent on robbery. We'd better get ready for 'em, just in case." He reached under the high seat and removed a double-barreled shotgun to hold it across his lap.

"Hyaah, get on up there," Cummins cried, slapping the reins on the rumps of the six mules pulling the wagon. He cursed fervently at the animals as they finally broke into a reluctant trot. "With these long-eared jackasses lugging us we sure can't outrun whoever's comin', so let's just hope they're peaceable."

"I'll go along with that," Corby agreed as he pulled the ancient Navy Colt he carried from the scarred leather holster on his right hip and checked its action. He squinted against the glaring late afternoon sun while he studied the rapidly nearing dust cloud. "Right now I'm guessing they're not aimin' to cause us any trouble. Whoever they are, they're not tryin' to hide their sign at all. They sure ain't Indians. No Comanches worth their salt would raise a cloud like that."

"I truly hope you're right, Ace," Cummins responded as they neared a low rise. "They're still too far away for me to make out who they might be. Well, I reckon we'll know who those riders are soon enough."

Moments later, both men breathed sighs of relief when a group of blue-clad riders topped the ridge, a cavalry guidon flapping in the breeze as the column of troopers approached at a brisk trot.

"Whoa there, you useless flop-eared flea-bitten excuses for mules." With a blistering oath, Cummins pulled back on his reins to jerk his team to a halt. He and his partner sat waiting as the soldiers approached.

"Column, halt!" Hand raised, the officer at the head of the patrol ordered his men to a stop when they reached the pair of teamsters. He studied the freighters carefully before greeting them.

"Good afternoon, gentlemen. Where are you headed?"

"Howdy to yourself, Major," Cummins cheerfully returned the greeting. "I'm Jeb Cummins, and this here ugly lookin' hombre is my pardner, Ace Corby. We're running a load of freight up to Monterey and Lubbock. And we're sure glad to see you boys out here. We thought for a minute you might be a pack of road agents on our tail."

"Or maybe a bunch of renegade Comanches who jumped the reservation," Corby added.

"We're hardly road agents. I'm Major Thaddeus Saunders, in charge of this patrol," the officer answered, with a disarming smile. He sat ramrod straight in the saddle, his close-cropped hair and neatly trimmed mustache a salt-and-pepper gray, his eyes an opaque steel gray to match. He continued in a clipped Eastern accent. "But there are plenty of highwaymen in this area preying on honest men like yourselves. That's why we're out here, to protect the citizenry from outlaws and raiding Indians who have left the Territory reservations."

"Have you seen any of those right around these parts lately?" Corby asked.

"No, we haven't," Saunders reluctantly admitted. "But I would still advise you to use the utmost caution."

"We always do," Cummins replied, "Now once you soldier boys go on by we can be on our way."

"We're going to take a short rest here and give our horses a breather, so once we move aside the trail will be all yours," Saunders answered.

"We appreciate that," Cummins replied. He held his team in check as the soldiers reined their horses to the side of the road.

Once the freighters had passed the troop, the two rearmost soldiers pulled their rifles from their saddle scabbards, raised them to their shoulders, and took careful aim. Cummins and Corby toppled from their seat to lie sprawled in the dust as a bullet slammed into each of their backs.

"Good work, men," Major Saunders stated. "Now hurry and get those bodies and wagon off the road. We'll bury those men and cache the cargo tonight, once it's good and dark. Those rifles they were hauling will bring a good price in the Territories. And I'm sure we'll have no trouble peddling the rest of the goods."

❀   ❀   ❀

Two days later and twenty miles to the northwest, the erstwhile cavalry patrol was just approaching a sharp curve which skirted a high bluff on the trail to Throckmorton. At this spot the trail threaded its way through a narrow arroyo, providing a perfect spot for an ambush. Major Thaddeus Saunders had carefully chosen the bluff for an attack on the Throckmorton stage … but the coach had already passed.

"The blasted stage is way ahead of schedule," Saunders cursed, eyeing a column of dust rapidly fading into the distance.

"We can still catch up to it, Major," Jeremiah Duffy, a stocky trooper wearing sergeant's chevrons, pointed out.

"You're right, Duffy," Saunders agreed with his chief aide. "Let's ride!" With a wave of his hand, Saunders ordered the column of troopers down the slope and onto the trail at a hard gallop.

Hearing the hoofbeats of rapidly approaching horses, the stage's driver and shotgun guard cast worried glances back over their shoulders at the pursuing riders who'd seemingly appeared out of nowhere. Their brief moment of relief at spotting the blue-clad troopers' uniforms quickly turned to panic as several of the nearest soldiers opened fire, hoping to quickly strike down the two men. With accurate shooting from the back of a galloping horse virtually impossible, the shots went wild.

With the soldiers rapidly closing, the driver slapped the reins hard across the rumps of his team, sending the horses racing ahead. The guard clambered onto the roof of the violently rocking Concord and flattened himself on his belly amidst the luggage and boxes strapped there. Lead punched through his flimsy cover as he aimed his shotgun at the nearest trooper and pulled the trigger of one barrel. The trooper shrieked as he took the load of buckshot in his chest and stomach and was knocked backwards from his saddle, rolling over several times in the dust before lying face down and unmoving.

The guard suddenly jerked upward as a lucky shot took him in the center of his chest. He grabbed futilely at a suitcase as the coach jounced roughly over a pothole. The dying man's upper body slumped over the side of the stage, dangling there for a moment until the Concord jolted violently over another rut, tossing the guard into a roadside ditch.

The three passengers inside the coach had unlimbered their guns and began blazing away at the raiders, with little effect. As the soldiers closed in on the stage, bullets pierced the thin wooden paneling of the Concord. One struck a whiskey drummer square in his face, knocking him back in his seat before he slid lifelessly to the floor.

When the pursuing troopers fired a ragged volley, the stage driver let out a low grunt as several bullets took him in his back. Mortally hit, he tumbled out of his seat and thudded to the road. With the driver's tight grip on the reins released, the panicked horses raced forward at even greater speed until two of the soldiers caught up with the team, grabbing the leaders' harnesses and dragging them to a halt. The rest of the cavalrymen surrounded the stage as it shuddered to a stop.

"Everyone out!" Saunders ordered as one of his men jumped from his horse and jerked open the coach door. "And keep your hands high. If anyone makes a move for his gun he'll die right now!"

The two surviving passengers, a grizzled cowpuncher and a young school teacher on his way to a new assignment in the Indian Territories emerged, hands held well above their shoulders.

"What the devil is this all about?" the cowboy demanded as he glared defiantly at Saunders and his men.

"It's quite simple, really," Saunders replied. "It's a robbery. This coach is carrying quite a load of gold double eagles for the bank in Throckmorton. My men and I intend to put that money to better use. We'll also be relieving you of any valuables you may be carrying."

Efficiently, several of Saunders' men went through the passengers' pockets, removing their wallets, and a gold watch from the teacher's vest.

"Please don't take this personally," Saunders' mouth twisted in a malicious grin, "But we can't afford to leave any witnesses."

The cowboy grabbed for his sixgun, having no chance as one of the soldiers put two bullets into his belly. Clutching at his middle, the mortally wounded cowpuncher doubled over, rolling onto his side as he jackknifed to the dirt.

"Don't, please," the teacher futilely pleaded, his cry cut short as he was slammed against the side of the coach by a bullet through his heart. He hung there for a moment, then crumpled.

"Hurry up before someone happens along," Saunders ordered. "Duffy, Thornton, get that strongbox down and blast it open." The two chosen men clambered to the driver's seat, then reached under it to pull out the heavy strongbox and toss it to the road. Saunders aimed at the lock and fired, cursing when it resisted his first bullet. He fired again, and the lock yielded as the slug pierced its workings.

"Look at all that dinero," Matt Thornton exclaimed, as he flipped open the strongbox's lid and gazed greedily at the carefully stacked moneybags inside it.

"You can admire it later," Saunders snapped, "Right now just get it out of that box and into our saddlebags." Swiftly, the major's orders were complied with, the heavy sacks of twenty dollar gold pieces distributed evenly to assure each mount carried equal weight.

As the last canvas sack disappeared into a saddlebag Saunders ordered, "A couple of you pick up what's left of Rivera and tie him on his horse. Then let's get moving."

"What about the stagecoach?" Sergeant Duffy questioned. "Shouldn't we get rid of it somehow?"

"No, we don't have to worry about that," Saunders answered. "We've left no witnesses, and by the time anyone finds that coach we'll be miles away. Just get Rivera and mount up." Within minutes, the soldiers had swept out of sight, leaving the Concord abandoned in the road.

Two hours later, a lone cowboy drifting toward the Texas Panhandle in hopes of finding employment on one of the large ranches springing up on its grassy plains came upon the grim scene of the robbery. He reined in his nervously prancing gray, then swung from the saddle, lifting his Colt from its holster as he approached the bullet riddled stage.

"Take it easy, Spook," the rider soothed his mount as the gelding whinnied anxiously, shying at the sight and smell of blood. "Let's see if we can help these folks, not that it appears there's much chance of that."

The cowboy's face set in bleak anger as he examined the victims of the robbery, finding no signs of life in the shotgun guard, driver, or teacher. He glanced inside the coach to see the body of the whiskey drummer lying wedged between the seats.

"Whoever the no-good renegades are that robbed this stage, they didn't give any of these folks a chance, Spook," he remarked to his horse. "I guess the only thing I can do for them now is load 'em in the coach and bring them to town. I reckon I'd better tie you while I take care of that chore."

As he led his horse toward a stunted pin oak, the cowboy whirled around at the sound of a low moan coming from a cluster of boulders scattered alongside the road. For the first time he noticed the thin trail of still damp blood leading from the road to those rocks. He quickly tied his horse to the oak, then headed for the rock nest.

His Colt held at the ready, the cowboy cautiously eased his way around the boulders. He stopped short at the sight of a grizzled old cowpuncher slumped against the largest boulder, both hands clamped tightly to his blood-soaked middle. The old man tried vainly to lift the pistol in his lap as he eyed the approaching newcomer.

"Don't try for your gun," the cowboy urged, "I'm gonna try and help you. Just take it easy until I see what I can do."

"It's too late for that. There ain't a thing you can do for me," the oldster choked out. "I'm gutshot. Got two slugs in my belly. I figure I've played out my string. Water. Please, can you get me some water, mister?"

"I surely can," the cowboy softly replied, "I'll be right back." He hurried to his horse and lifted the canteen from his saddlehorn. Returning to the old cowpuncher, he knelt alongside him, unscrewed the top from his canteen and placed it to the his lips. The dying man choked as he took a long swallow of water.

"Thanks. Thanks, mister," he gasped. As a convulsion wracked his body, he suddenly exclaimed, "Army ... The Army."

The cowboy leaned closer. "What's that you're saying, old-timer? Do you want the Army?"

"No. No!" The old man shook his head. "The Army did ... did ..." His voice failed as his body shuddered and went slack.

CHAPTER 2

❀

"Sam, for the hundredth time, get out of here, doggone it! I sure don't need any help from you," Texas Ranger Lieutenant Jim Blawcyzk ordered his big paint gelding. Home on one of his infrequent and always too short leaves from the Rangers, Jim was trying to catch up on some of the neglected chores on the JB Bar, the small horse ranch he owned in the little town of San Leanna, not far from Austin. As he repaired the fence around Sam's corral, the horse kept nuzzling him insistently for attention. "I'm just about finished here, then I've got to get repair those boards on the back of your barn. Now get!" When Jim ordered him away, Sam snorted indignantly as he trotted to the other side of the corral.

"There. I'm finally about done here," Jim exclaimed with satisfaction as a short while later he nailed the last fence board in place. He looked up smiling as the sounds of two boys playing cowboys and Indians drifted across the yard. A moment later his eight year old son Charlie and Charlie's best friend Joe Deavers raced into view, banging away at each other with the rusted old Colts they carried. Chip, Charlie's collie, barked joyfully as he chased after the boys. They ran up to Jim and slid to a halt.

"Dad. Can me and Joe go swimmin'?" Charlie excitedly asked. "It's awful hot."

"You mean may Joe and I go swimming?" Jim smiled as he gently corrected his towheaded son. Charlie's blue eyes and blonde hair were exact matches for his father's. "And I don't know. Did you clean out the stalls?"

"Aw, Dad, you know I did that this morning," Charlie protested, "And since Joe's stayin' the night, we don't have to worry about being back so he can get home in time for supper."

"What about Ted?" Jim asked, referring to Charlie's pet buckskin paint gelding. "Has he been brushed?"

"Joe and I brushed him before we started playin' cowboys," Charlie complained. "C'mon Dad, you know that!"

"I know," Jim grinned, as was his habit fondly tousling his son's hair. "I'm just teasing you. Of course you can go swimming. I sure wish I could join you."

"Why don't you come swimmin' with us, Ranger Blawcyzk?" Joe urged. "That cool water's sure gonna feel mighty good."

"I'd like that well enough, but I've got too much to get done around here," Jim explained, "And I'm likely to hear from Headquarters any day now with new orders. You two just go on ahead and enjoy yourselves. Make sure to be home in time for supper, or your mom will skin all of us alive. You know she'll be back from the church a little later this afternoon. And that reminds me, Charlie. You'd better study your Catechism lesson before you take that swim."

"Aw, Dad, can't that wait?" Charlie cried with chagrin. "Besides, what would Joe do while I'm studying?"

"Of course it can wait," Jim chuckled. "As long as you know the lesson by Sunday. Now get out of here so I can get back to work."

"Gee, thanks Dad!" Charlie exclaimed. A minute later, both boys and the collie had disappeared from sight as they headed for the swimming hole in the clear stream which traversed the JB Bar.

"I reckon it's time to get at that barn wall," Jim sighed as he watched until the boys topped the rise behind the horse corrals. He stopped at the pump to take a long drink of water before he headed around the back of the stable. Jim paused to unbuckle his gunbelt and peel off his sweat soaked shirt to hang them from a protruding nail before he began to pry rotted planks from the wall.

Jim worked steadily for several hours, until the sound of an approaching horse and carriage came to his ears.

"That'll be Julia and Hattie Flannery comin' home from the church supper committee meeting," Jim thought, as he heard the carriage roll to a stop in his dusty front yard. "Well, I'll be finishing up here just about the time she has our own supper ready." He picked up his hammer and resumed nailing a board to the barn wall.

"Jim! Jim, where are you?" his wife Julia called a few minutes later. "Jim?"

"I'm back here, Julia. Behind the barn," Jim called back. It only took a moment for his wife to appear. Julia was a petite brunette, not a spectacular beauty, but wholesomely pretty. Her deep brown eyes always seemed to sparkle with laughter, except when Jim was leaving on an assignment. Her dark features, which contrasted with her husband's fair hair and blue eyes, made she and Jim a handsome couple indeed.

Julia walked up to Jim and kissed him on the cheek, letting her hand drift through the thick blonde hair covering his chest.

"Hattie Flannery sent you these," she told him, as she handed Jim a jar of peach preserves.

"Hattie didn't have to send those along now," Jim answered, "I could have gotten them when we stopped by to visit her and Tom on the way home from Mass on Sunday."

"Hattie knows full well, just like you and I do, that you'll probably have orders and be on the trail before Sunday gets here," Julia retorted. "That's why she sent them along now."

"I guess that makes sense," Jim agreed. "Well, if she's right and I'm gone then give her my thanks."

"I already have," Julia smiled. "I'll start getting supper ready. Where are Charlie and Joe?"

"They headed for the swimmin' hole a couple of hours ago," Jim explained, as he pulled the bandanna from his neck to wipe sweat from his face and chest. "I sure can't blame them in this heat. In fact, if I get this wall finished in time, I just might take a swim myself before supper." He smiled as he added, "Maybe I could even talk you into joining me."

"Not with Charlie and Joe around," Julia musically laughed. "But hold that thought, Ranger. Perhaps tomorrow." Her eyes held a definite promise as she kissed Jim once again, then headed for the house.

❧   ❧   ❧

Texas Ranger Corporal Smoky McCue was relaxed in his saddle, having just finished one of the cigarettes he always seemed to have dangling from his lips. As his dark gray gelding Soot trotted briskly along, the shrill war cries of Comanche warriors suddenly echoed across the rolling plain. With little warning, two half-naked braves raced out of the brush and descended on horse and rider, shooting wildly at the Ranger. Smoky, hands clutching his chest and belly, toppled from the saddle, rolled onto his back as he struck the ground, moaned once, then lay motionless.

"We got him, Running Wolf," one of the Comanches shouted triumphantly.

"We sure did. Now we've got to scalp him, Blue Eagle," the other replied as they walked up to Smoky's still form.

"Nobody's about to scalp me, especially not you two renegades," Smoky snarled as he jerked to a sitting position and yanked his pistol from its holster. "Got you both …" The Comanches spun to the ground as Smoky cut them down. The Ranger rose to his feet and stalked over to where they lay sprawled in the dust.

"I'm going to teach you two savages a lesson," Smoky growled as bending down he picked up the bodies of the two Indians, tucking one under each arm.

"Uncle Smoky, no! Let us go!" Charlie yelped, as Smoky grabbed them. Since he was a toddler, Charlie had known his father's riding partner and best friend as his "Uncle Smoky". Giggling uncontrollably, Charlie and Joe, the two "Comanches", struggled futilely to break McCue's grip. Effortlessly he carried them over to where Soot stood waiting patiently and swung them both up onto the horse's broad back, Charlie in front of the saddle and Joe behind.

"C'mon. You're coming with me. No good ambushing renegades," Smoky grumbled in mock anger as he climbed into the saddle and pushed Soot into a trot toward the Blawcyzk ranch house.

Jim and Julia were relaxing on the front porch of their neatly white-washed house, enjoying glasses of cool lemonade when Smoky rode into the yard. They watched curiously as Jim's Ranger partner rode up to the steps.

"Howdy, Jim. Hello, Julia. I found me a couple of Comanche raiders right outside your gate, pard," Smoky announced as he reined Soot to a halt.

"You should've just drilled 'em and been done with it, Smoke," Jim laughed as Smoky lowered the boys to the ground and swung from his saddle. "And I'll bet I can guess what brings you by. You've been to Headquarters."

"Nope," Smoky disagreed, "Cap'n Trumbull sent a messenger to track me down."

"That couldn't have been too hard," Jim laughed. "All he'd have to do is look in the Silver Star Saloon. That's where you're bound to be whenever you're in Austin."

"You're right," Smoky conceded. "And you'd also be right if you said we had orders. We do."

"Well, you can tell me about them while you take care of your horse and clean up some," Jim said.

"Speaking of cleaning up, Charlie, you and Joe wash up. It's nearly suppertime," Julia put in. "And both of you make sure your hands are clean, or Joe won't get to stay the night," she warned.

"Aww, Mom …" Charlie began to protest.

"Hey, you listen to your mom, or you won't get to see the surprise I've got in my saddlebags for you … and Joe," Smoky ordered.

"All right, Uncle Smoky," Charlie readily agreed.

"And you'll be staying here tonight, won't you, Smoky?" Julia anxiously asked. "I hope you and Jim won't have to ride out until morning."

"I reckon that will be okay, as long as it's all right with Jim," Smoky replied.

"You know it is, Smoke," Jim agreed. "C'mon, you can let me know where we're headed while you take care of Soot and wash up."

"Sure," McCue agreed. "I'll have Jim back to you in a few minutes, Julia."

"Supper will be ready when you are," Julia smiled. "I noticed you managed to show up right in time for supper, Smoky … not that I'm at all surprised by your timing. I hope chicken and dumplings with apple cobbler for dessert will suit you."

"They'll suit me just fine," Smoky grinned. "Let's go, Jim. The faster I clean up the faster I can get at that chicken."

Smoky waited until they were in the barn and out of Julia's earshot before telling Jim the little information he had been provided from Captain Trumbull.

"Jim, I didn't want to say anything in front of Julia about our orders," Smoky began, "A Ranger's wife has enough to worry about anyway, and I'm not sure how you'd want to break this news to her."

"What do you mean, pard?" Jim asked, clearly puzzled.

"I don't know what our orders are or where we'll be headed," Smoky explained. "Whatever the Captain's got in store for us must be really hush-hush. The only thing that messenger told me was for you and I to report to Captain Trumbull the first thing in the morning. I wasn't sure how you'd want to break that news to your wife."

"That is kind of strange," Jim agreed. "But Julia will understand. We've been through this often enough. You sure there's nothing else?"

"That's all, Jim," Smoke reiterated. "Right now, you know just as much as I do."

Smoky finished caring for his horse, then turned the steeldust out in the corral with Jim's paint. The two men headed for the pump and wash bench in back of the house, stripping off their shirts and dunking their heads into the cold water of the trough.

"Are you two just about ready?" Julia called from the house. "If you don't hurry I'll just let Charlie and Joe eat all your supper."

"She means it, too, Smoke," Jim chuckled to his partner. More loudly, he called, "We'll be right there, darling." Both men hurriedly finished washing and toweling off, shrugging into their shirts as they headed for the kitchen.

Later that evening, with Charlie and Joe spending the night sleeping in the hayloft along with Smoky, who would entertain the boys with his greatly exaggerated war stories, Jim and Julia lay side by side in their bed.

"Jim, are you sure that's all Smoky told you?" Julia questioned, "Are you positive you're not holding something back to try and protect me?"

"Absolutely," Jim answered. "That's all Captain Trumbull said. And I've never kept anything from you since we've been married, have I? I made that promise to you the day we were wed."

"I know you haven't, and I know you never will," Julia agreed. "Still, it is rather strange of Captain Trumbull not to at least tell you where you are headed."

"I know," Jim conceded, "But once Smoky and I meet with him in the morning I'll either come back here and tell you where we're bound, or get word to you if we have to ride straight out."

"That all I ask," Julia agreed. She rolled onto her side to place her lips to his.

Jim enfolded Julia in his arms as they embraced in the embrace of two people greatly in love, who knew not when, or even if, they would be together again.

CHAPTER 3

As was their usual habit, Jim and Smoky arose well before sunrise the next morning. While they fed and groomed their horses and Jim filled his saddlebags with needed supplies for the trail, Julia cooked them a huge farewell breakfast. Sam and Soot were contentedly munching their oats when their riders headed back to the house for their own morning meal.

"Charlie, don't forget to say Grace," Jim reminded his son as they settled at the table, which was nearly sagging under the weight of platters piled high with ham, bacon, eggs, hotcakes, and biscuits, accompanied by freshly-churned butter, homemade preserves, and thick molasses. A pot of strong black coffee steamed on top of the stove.

"All right, Dad," Charlie responded, bowing his head. "Bless us O Lord, and these Thy gifts, which we are about to receive from Thy bounty, through Christ our Lord. Amen. Now can we eat?"

"Go ahead," Jim chuckled, as Charlie stabbed several hotcakes with his fork. The kitchen fell nearly silent while they worked on the meal.

When they were finished, Joe thanked Julia, saying, "That sure was good, Mrs. Blawcyzk. Thanks."

"You're welcome, Joe," Julia replied.

"I've got to agree with Joe. That was indeed a delicious breakfast, as always Julia," Smoky praised as he pushed himself back from the table and patted his full belly. "And it's especially appreciated since the only cookin' I'll most likely have to look forward to for the next several days is your husband's campfire bacon and beans."

"I never noticed you turnin' 'em down, Smoke," Jim retorted. "And you put enough away this morning I shouldn't have to feed you for a week anyway. Poor ol' Soot's liable to get a swayback when you climb into the saddle … if he can even carry you at all."

"Smoky, if you'd find yourself a good woman to marry, then you wouldn't have to worry about eating in saloons or greasy cafes all the time," Julia sweetly added. Unable to resist teasing him just a bit more she added, "And perhaps Jim and I could eat at your house then, for a change."

Smoky hastily arose from his chair, blushing and quickly stating, "Jim, we'd better get riding. We don't want to keep Captain Trumbull waiting."

"There you go, Julia," Jim laughed. "You've scared him off again with that talk of marriage. All right Smoke, we'll head on out."

"Julia, would you like our help with the dishes before we leave?" Smoky politely asked.

"No," Julia answered, "Jim's broken enough of my china when he's tried to help clean up the kitchen. Besides, I have Charlie and Joe to give me a hand." Before the two boys could even begin to protest, she added, "And once the dishes are done I can start baking oatmeal cookies. Smoky, you and Jim just leave things as they are and go saddle your horses. I'll join you in a few minutes."

Jim and Smoky headed for the barn, where Sam, Soot, Charlie's pet gelding Ted, and Joe's bay Wyoming were just finishing their morning rations of hay. Sam whickered his eagerness to travel as Jim entered the barn. When Jim opened the paint's stall door, Sam nuzzled his chest, then dropped his head to Jim's hip pocket, begging for the peppermint Jim always kept there.

"All right, of course you can have your candy," Jim laughed as he dug out a peppermint and slipped it to the horse. While Sam crunched on the treat, Jim threw the saddle on his back and tightened the cinches. Once their horses' bridles were in place, Jim and Smoky led the mounts into the yard. Julia stood waiting at the bottom of the porch steps, holding two wrapped packages in her hands. Charlie and Joe stood at her side.

"I packed you boys some extra food for the trail, as always," Julia stated as she handed each of them a packet.

"That means I won't have to eat Jim's cookin' for a couple more days anyway," Smoky chuckled as he climbed into his saddle. "Thanks, Julia."

Jim hugged his son as he told him, "Charlie, you be sure and listen to your mom, and make certain all your chores are done. You know I depend on you to help out around here while I'm gone."

"I know, Dad. You can count on me." Charlie assured him.

"And I'll help too when I can," Joe piped up.

"Thanks, Joe. I appreciate that," Jim replied. "Charlie, don't forget you're one of the altar boys at Mass this week."

"I won't," Charlie promised. "Dad, make sure and take care of yourself."

"That's a promise," Jim answered as he fondly tousled Charlie's hair. Jim then turned to his wife.

"Jim, please be careful. I promise not to worry about you … at least not too much," Julia half-whispered.

"I always am, aren't I?" Jim fibbed, for he knew, as did Julia, the chances he took to enforce the law as a Texas Ranger. "Don't fret about me. I'll be fine."

"I know you will," Julia answered as Jim took her in his arms for a long, lingering kiss. They only broke their embrace when Smoky discreetly coughed as he gazed at the horizon.

"We've got to get moving, pard," Smoky softly said.

"All right," Jim agreed as he swung onto Sam's back, "Julia, I'll be back in a few weeks."

"Make sure you are … and in one piece," Julia answered. "Don't come home to me with any holes in that handsome hide of yours, Ranger."

"Handsome, hah!" Smoky chortled, his laughter quickly subsiding as Julia glared at him in feigned anger. "Now I know we'd better ride, Jim, before I get shot right here!"

"Then let's get going." Jim dug his bootheels into Sam's sides, sending the paint forward at a brisk walk, Smoky and Soot alongside. The sun was just topping the eastern horizon as the partners rode out of the JB Bar yard.

❧   ❧   ❧

Ninety minutes later, Jim and Smoky reined up in front of Texas Ranger Headquarters in Austin. They looped their horses' reins over the tooth-marked hitchrail in front of the low roofed building and loosened their cinches before heading inside.

The partners pushed open the front door and walked past the reception office, which was still empty at this early hour. They headed down a long, wainscoted corridor to the cramped office of their commanding officer, Captain Hank Trumbull. Trumbull was gazing pensively out his window, but turned to greet his two veteran Rangers as he heard their footsteps just outside his door.

"Jim, Smoky. Thank you for getting here at this ungodly hour," Trumbull greeted them. The captain was a bulldog of a man, barrel chested and still muscular, even though he was well into his fifties. His hair had gone gray, but his frosty blue eyes could still seem to pierce right through a man. He waved at a battered pot on the stove in a corner of the room. "Help yourselves to coffee if you want. Jim, how's the family?"

"Thanks, Cap'n," Jim answered, as he took two tin mugs off a shelf and poured them brim full of the steaming brew, passing one to Smoky. "Julia and Charlie are doing just fine. Julia said to tell you she'll be sending you some of her oatmeal cookies the next time I'm home. Thank you for asking."

"I'll look forward to those cookies, Jim. Now you boys pull yourselves up a chair while I get out some files," Trumbull invited. While the captain dug through a cabinet behind his desk, Jim settled into a corner chair, leaning back against the wall as Smoky took a seat opposite Trumbull's desk. Smoky rolled and lighted a quirly as they waited.

"I know you both must be curious as to what this assignment will involve, since I was unable to give Smoky very much information," Trumbull began as he settled behind his cluttered, scarred desk and filled his pipe. He touched a match to the bowl, puffing until he was satisfied the tobacco was burning steadily. He leaned back in his chair and blew a ring of smoke toward the ceiling, narrowly eyeing the men awaiting their orders.

"I reckon you could say that, Cap'n," Jim softly replied.

"You'll know in a moment why I had to be so secretive," Trumbull answered as he dropped his feet to the floor and opened one of the thick folders he had scattered on his desk.

"Jim, Smoky, there've been a lot of reports of robberies and killings coming in from up in north Texas, anywhere from Abilene up into the Panhandle," Trumbull began. "There's also been some cattle rustlin' and horse thievin' going on for good measure."

"Beggin' your pardon, but that's nothing unusual, Cap'n," Smoky stated. "That's pretty wild country up that way, and the population is really sparse. Add in the fact it's so close to the Territories that renegades both red and white can jump the border real easy and it's made to order for outlaws."

"Everything you say is true, Ranger," Trumbull agreed. "Except there seem to be a lot more crimes being committed than usual. Here, take a look." He passed the folder to Smoky, who studied it for a moment, then passed it to Jim. Jim perused its contents, then let out a low whistle.

"I see what you mean, Cap'n." Jim said, "From what I've read here, this is far more than the occasional bank or stage robbery pulled off by border hopping desperadoes. It appears that we might have a new gang to contend with."

"You're absolutely right, Jim. These files are full of reports of stagecoach and freight wagon robberies," Trumbull agreed. "And in every instance there were no witnesses left alive. Unfortunately, it appears we're dealing with cold-blooded murderers."

"Aren't there any clues as to who might be behind these robberies?" Smoky questioned.

"There's only one, and it's a mighty slim one," Trumbull replied. "Plus once I reveal it you'll see the reason why I didn't want to say anything until you were here in my office."

"We're waiting, Captain," Jim replied, rather impatiently.

Trumbull took another long draw on his pipe before continuing.

"There was a robbery of the Butterfield stage to Throckmorton. Ten thousand dollars in gold double eagles was taken, in addition to whatever valuables the passengers carried. As usual, whoever robbed the stage gunned down the driver, shotgun guard, and the passengers, in this case three of them."

"So there were no witnesses left alive," Smoky interrupted.

"Just let me finish," Trumbull rejoined. "In this case there was a witness, an old cowhand the robbers shot and left for dead. However, he lived for a while. He was still breathing when a cowboy rode up on the coach. He said a few words before he died." Trumbull hesitated before he opened another file and continued, reading from its contents.

"That cowhand's last words were, 'Army. The Army,' then 'Army. Army did …'".

"That's it?" Jim asked.

"That's all," Trumbull confirmed. "We have no idea whether that man meant he'd been in the Army, he had seen an Army patrol, or was talking about an Army post."

"Or that the Army was somehow involved in the robbery of that stage," Jim concluded.

"That's entirely correct, Jim," Trumbull answered. "So you see what our dilemma is. Things are still tense between the Federal and State authorities. It hasn't been all that many years since Reconstruction ended. We can't just charge in and risk antagonizing the U.S. Army, even if some of their soldiers are somehow involved. We can't chance giving the Federal authorities an excuse to reimpose martial law. The carpetbaggers have barely been cleared out of Texas, and we sure don't need them back again."

"Plus we have no proof that even if those appeared to be soldiers who robbed that coach they actually were," Smoky added. "They could be renegades disguising themselves as cavalrymen, or maybe even deserters."

"Precisely," Trumbull agreed. "So you and Jim need to figure out exactly who is pulling off these robberies and murders before you make any accusations."

"Well, whoever it is, we'll be dealing with some *muy malo hombres*," Jim observed.

"I couldn't agree more," Trumbull answered. "With the cattle trails up there, the buffalo hunters, renegades in general, and new settlers pouring in, more law is needed up that way in any event. The Army has their forts, but they're charged with dealing with the Indians, not with Texas citizens, although they do their share of law enforcement when necessary. Things are bad enough up there I was planning on sending a troop up there as soon as possible in any event. I'd hoped to send Jim Huggins and some men from Company C up there last month, but C is still tied up with that trouble along the Border, so it's up to you and Smoky. I'll be honest. This is probably the most dangerous assignment I've ever handed you. If you back out I won't blame you, and there will be no questions asked. So what do you say? Will you take on this mission?"

"I haven't been up to the Panhandle for quite a while, Cap'n," Jim replied, "I reckon it's high time I see it again."

"Same here," Smoky added. "We'll get to the bottom of this for you, Cap'n. I've got just one question, though."

"What's that?" Trumbull asked.

"Do you have any idea where we should start looking for those hombres?"

"I wish I did, but I haven't got a clue," Trumbull frankly replied. "From the reports we've received, that gang ranges pretty much all over up there, from Abilene up into the Panhandle. They don't seem to be following any set pattern, so we have no idea where they'll hit next. You'll just have to follow your instincts."

"How about any local lawmen we could contact?" Jim asked. "Are there any sheriffs or town marshals you know of that might help?"

"Not really," Trumbull shrugged. "A few of the settlements up there might have appointed themselves a marshal, but I don't know any of them. Since you can't count on much, if any, cooperation from the Army, you'll be pretty much on your own. And I don't have to tell you that's a big amount of territory to cover."

"Then we've got a lot of ridin' ahead of us," Jim answered, "But we'll find those renegades. You can bet a hat on it."

"I appreciate that, both of you," Trumbull gratefully replied. "And of course if you run across any other outlaws you'll bring them in too. Make sure you have your Fugitive Lists with you, since it's likely you'll come across a few men on the run from us up in that territory," As he rose from his chair the captain concluded, "And whatever you do, you'll have to be certain that you're extremely diplomatic in your dealings with the Army."

"Tact is my middle name, Cap'n," Jim answered, ignoring the look of incredulity Smoky shot him.

"Sure it is, Lieutenant," Trumbull sarcastically retorted. "Now, before I say anything further about your 'tactful nature' … Is there anything either of you will need before you leave?"

"Just let Julia know where I'm bound," Jim answered as he stood up, drained the dregs from his mug, and placed it on the shelf.

"I'll do that," Trumbull promised. "In fact, I'll ride over to your place later this mornin' and tell her personally."

"You're only using that as an excuse to get your hands on some of her oatmeal cookies," Jim chuckled.

"I can't put one over on you, can I Lieutenant?" Trumbull retorted with a laugh.

"Not when it's that obvious, Cap'n," Jim grinned. "I reckon we'll be ridin.'"

"I don't need to tell both of you to be careful," Trumbull stated as he shook both men's hands. "I sure don't want to have to replace two of my best Rangers."

"We kind of feel that way too, Cap'n," Smoky answered. "*Adios.*"

"*Vaya con Dios*," Trumbull stated, "Send me a report once you know anything."

"We'll do our best," Jim promised.

Trumbull watched morosely from his window as Jim and Smoky tightened their cinches and climbed into their saddles, then headed their horses down Congress Avenue at a lope.

"I certainly hope and pray I'm not sending those two into more trouble than they can handle," he thought. As Jim and Smoky rode from sight he turned from the window, pulled a tumbler and bottle of whiskey from his bottom desk drawer and filled the glass to its brim. He downed the liquor in one swallow then refilled the glass, sinking into his battered chair as he gloomily studied the amber liquid.

CHAPTER 4

To all outward appearances, Jim Blawcyzk and Smoky McCue were merely another two of the many grubline riding cowboys wandering across Texas from ranch to ranch as they rode steadily northward. Since Texas Rangers wore no uniforms there was nothing about their clothing or equipment to distinguish them from ordinary cowpunchers. However, while most Rangers didn't carry badges, Jim and Smoky had snugged in their shirt pockets silver star on silver circle badges, which they'd hand carved from Mexican ten peso coins. That insignia of Ranger authority was slowly becoming more widespread among the men who carried the law to the far reaches of the Lone Star State. The two lawmen would keep those badges out of sight until necessary.

While they had been riding partners for several years and were the best of friends, the two men couldn't have been more opposite in personality and appearance. Jim was tall and lanky, standing a shade over six feet tall without his boots and wide-brimmed hat, and fair, with a thatch of thick, unruly blonde hair under the tan Stetson that shaded his clear blue eyes. His face, while still retaining somewhat of a youthful appearance, had been weathered by years of exposure to the Texas sun and wind, making him appear older than his age of thirty-two. He favored brightly colored shirts and bandannas, which often led to his fellow Rangers kidding him that with those bright clothes he made a good target for outlaw bullets. A light brown cowhide vest and scuffed boots completed his outfit. There were no spurs attached to those boots, as Jim refused to ever put steel to a horse's flanks. Jim was left handed, so his heavy Colt Peacemaker, a revolver still fairly rare in Texas, hung at his left hip, while a Bowie knife was snugged in a sheath on his belt. Jim was reluctant to use that Colt and the Winchester riding in his saddle scabbard unless forced. Nevertheless, he was proficient in their use, and deadly accurate with his aim. While most Rangers were single, Jim was happily married and completely devoted to his wife and son. He was descended from the original group of Polish immigrants that had settled in the town of Bandera in the mid-1850's, which accounted for his somewhat unusual surname. A devout Catholic, Jim attended Sunday Mass whenever possible, and never drank, smoked, nor cursed. His quiet demeanor had fooled many a lawbreaker into underestimating him until it was too late. However, Jim did enjoy a good game of poker, which afforded him a much needed diversion while on the trail. He rode a big-boned, ill-tempered palomino paint gelding named Sam, a horse which only Jim could handle. Constant brushing kept Sam's yellow and white splotched coat shining like burnished gold.

Smoky McCue on the other hand was slightly shorter than average, but with a tough, wiry build, standing about five foot eight or nine in his boots. A year younger than Jim, Smoky had dark gray eyes, a pencil thin mustache, and black hair which had turned prematurely white at the tips, giving the illusion of a puff of smoke whenever he removed his battered black Stetson. It was this hair which had earned Smoky his nickname. His given name was unknown, since he had never revealed it to anyone, not even to Captain Trumbull or Jim. He preferred dark clothing, usually dressing in dark brown or black shirts, the only colorful item he wore a bright red bandanna draped loosely around his neck. His vest was of black leather, with a sack of tobacco and leaf of cigarette papers ever present in its left breast pocket. Even the gunbelt and holsters which carried his Colts and knife were of tooled black leather. Smoky was one of very few men who actually wore two sixguns, and he was equally proficient firing those pistols with either hand. Where Jim could be quiet to the point of being reserved, Smoky was loud and outgoing, always looking for a conversation or an argument. Unlike his partner, the smoke-haired McCue loved nothing so much as to spend an evening in the saloons when in town, drinking and gambling, preferably in the company of an attractive young saloon lady. Smoky also was constantly rolling and lighting quirlies, so he was rarely without a cigarette in his mouth. His family had been in Texas for generations, with several of his ancestors having taken part in the fight for Texas independence. Smoky's steeldust gelding Soot complemented his rider perfectly, the horse's charcoal gray coat and steady temper well-suited for a Ranger mount.

Despite their differences, Jim and Smoky had formed an instant bond when they'd first been assigned to the same Ranger company. Each had saved the other's life on more than one occasion as they and their fellow Rangers battled the renegades and outlaws swarming over the vast reaches and rugged land of the Lone Star State. Even when Jim had risen to the rank of Lieutenant, while McCue had only been promoted to Corporal, they rode together on their assignments whenever possible. Recognizing the pair's invaluable contributions to the Rangers, Captain Trumbull had eventually taken them from the company in which they rode and handed his toughest missions to them. Working on their own, Blawcyzk and McCue were able to ferret out lawbreakers who otherwise would have ridden away at the mere hint of a Ranger troop in the area.

By the time several days and nearly two hundred miles had passed, Jim and Smoky looked even more like down on their luck drifting cowpokes. Neither had shaved since leaving Austin, so their jaws wore thick coats of stubbled whiskers. Their clothing and horses were coated with the dust of those long miles. Both men and mounts had thinned down from the hard run toward the Texas Panhandle.

It was about two hours before sundown when Jim reined Sam to a halt on the banks of a shallow, clear stream.

"What're you stopping for, Jim?" Smoky demanded as he pulled Soot to a halt alongside his partner.

"I figured we'd give the horses a breather for a few minutes," Jim answered as he lifted his canteen from the saddlehorn and dismounted. His paint immediately dropped his nose to the creek and began sucking up water. Smoky's steeldust followed suit, thirstily taking in the cool liquid as his rider dismounted.

"What for?" Smoky questioned, as he pulled his cigarette papers and sack of tobacco from his vest pocket. "We'll be scoutin' out a place to camp pretty soon anyway. We could have just kept on ridin' until we put up for the night."

"No," Jim explained as he hunkered alongside the stream to fill his canteen. "I figure if we keep pushin' for another few hours we can make Swanson's trading post well before ten o'clock. There'll be enough of a moon after dusk to see the trail by, that is unless you're too tuckered out to keep going for that long."

"You know I can ride as long and as hard as you can, Lieutenant," Smoky indignantly replied. "We'll keep on until we reach Swanson's place." He dropped to his belly to take a long drink from the creek. "Boy, that does taste good," he stated in satisfaction as he finished.

"I knew you'd agree," Jim chuckled, "Especially since old Jack Swanson always has a big pot of beef stew simmering on the stove and whiskey behind the bar."

"Swanson's grub might taste awful, but it's still a welcome change from your bacon and beans, that's for dang certain," Smoky answered as he came to his feet and began to roll a quirly.

"I'll go along with you there, Smoke," Jim agreed. "Even I'm tired of the taste of my chuck at this point. And Swanson's grub doesn't taste all that bad since he started letting his wife do the cookin'. Besides, the horses will get a good graining there, which they can sure use. And we can pick up some supplies."

Smoky studied the sky critically as he took a drag on his cigarette.

"Jim, I don't mean to differ with you, but those clouds to the west look like they'll cover the moon well before we reach Swanson's," he pointed out.

"Those clouds aren't rollin' in that fast," Jim replied. "We'll take our chances, unless you've got any real objections."

"Not as long as you don't plan on bunking down in one of those flea-bitten cots Swanson has the nerve to call beds," Smoky retorted as he dug a lucifer from his vest pocket, thumbed it to life, and touched it to the end of his cigarette.

"There's not a chance of that," Jim laughed. "The first and only time I tried gettin' some shut-eye in that bunkhouse of Swanson's I lost more blood to those critters than I would have if I'd taken a bellyfull of buckshot from both barrels of a shotgun at close range. No, we'll just have the horses fed, buy those supplies, eat and have a couple of drinks, then bed down out back with Sam and Soot."

"Now you're making sense," Smoky said as he took a long pull on his cigarette. "And I wonder if Swanson still has those three good lookin' daughters of his working around the place ... not that I'm forgetting that real pretty Kiowa wife he's got either."

"I was wondering when you'd get around to those girls," Jim knowingly grinned. "Well, we won't find out about them just hanging around here all night."

"Try not to use the word 'hanging', Jim," Smoky gulped, reaching up to his neck to rub a faint scar still barely visible there, the result of a south Texas lynch mob's mistakenly identifying him as the killer of a woman some time back. Jim's timely arrival had saved McCue from dangling at the end of that mob's rope.

"Sorry, pard," Jim apologized. "I reckon these horses have had enough of a rest. Let's get movin'." He climbed back into the saddle and rehung his canteen. Smoky pulled himself onto Soot's back and flipped the butt of his cigarette into the creek.

"Let's go, Sam," Jim urged his paint, nudging him in the ribs. After letting the horses jog easily for a half mile, the Rangers once again urged their mounts into a ground-covering lope.

CHAPTER 5

"That'll be Swanson's place up ahead, about two miles or so. We'll be there in roughly half an hour," Jim noted a little more than five hours later, as he glimpsed a flicker of distant lamplight for just a moment. The Rangers had been riding non-stop since their brief rest alongside the nameless creek. They had been slowed somewhat for the past hour as despite Jim's earlier prediction the moon had disappeared behind a thickening cloud bank. Without its light, the horses had to pick their way cautiously along the rutted trail.

"And none too soon, either. I'm sure looking forward to a hot meal and a few drinks, and I'm just as certain Soot's eager to spend a night in a comfortable stall," Smoky replied as he shifted around stiffly to make himself more comfortable in the saddle. While he was an expert, almost tireless horseman, as were all the Rangers, there were very few men in the organization who could ride as long or hard as his partner, despite Smoky's unwillingness to concede that. There were still fewer Rangers' horses which had the speed and endurance of Blawcyzk's paint. However, even Sam was beginning to show signs of weariness after this longest day so far of the journey north, while Soot's head was hanging low in exhaustion.

"Maybe we'll sleep in a bit tomorrow morning," Jim answered. "Perhaps even as late as an hour past sunup."

"You're all heart, Lieutenant," Smoky laughed.

As the buildings that comprised Swanson's Trading Post came into sight Sam and Soot, despite their weariness, broke into a shuffling jog as they sensed food, water, and rest ahead.

"Take it easy, Sam," Jim urged his gelding. "You'll be settled in soon enough."

Swanson's was a ramshackle, hastily built complex that sprawled alongside a bend in a good sized stream known as Parson's Creek. Jack Swanson, the proprietor, had chosen the location for his business because of the cottonwoods along the creek, which provided welcome shade in this virtually treeless section of Texas. The main building was constructed of whatever materials had been handy. A sagging front porch ran its entire width, and the whole structure had been so haphazardly thrown together it looked on the verge of collapse. It held the trading post, barroom, and the Swanson family's living quarters. Behind it was a shabby bunkhouse containing a few straw tick mattresses where travelers could rest overnight, as well as a leanto barn and corrals for their horses. Except for a small circle of light spilling from a lantern onto the front porch, the entire place was hidden in deep shadow as the Rangers approached.

After days on the trail Jim and Smoky were dead tired and nowhere near as alert as they normally would be, especially after spending close to sixteen hours in the saddle this day. They rode up to the hitchrail in front of Swanson's and stiffly dismounted.

"Howdy, fellas," a grizzled, buckskin clad buffalo hunter greeted them from where he sat whittling on the porch. "Sure is a nice evenin', ain't it?" He spat a thick stream of tobacco juice into the dust.

"It sure is," Jim agreed as he looped his reins over the rail, stumbling a bit as Sam nosed him in the middle of his back. "You just wait a few minutes, Sam," Jim scolded his horse as the paint nuzzled at his hip pocket for a peppermint. "You'll be fed in a little while."

Jim was too late to react at a slight sound behind him. He started to whirl, only to be stopped in his tracks by the barrel of a Colt digging into his spine.

"We'll take care of those horses for you," a harsh voice behind Jim grated. "Don't even think of turning around. Just keep your hands away from your gun and step away from that paint. Turn around slow so I can keep an eye on you."

"Don't try it, unless you want a bullet through your guts," another man warned as Smoky reached for the Colt on his hip. Smoky raised his hands shoulder high as the speaker emerged from the shadows with his sixgun leveled at McCue's belt buckle.

"I wouldn't try stealin' my horse," Jim warned as he raised his hands over his head, then backed away from Sam's side and turned to face his assailant. "He won't take kindly to it."

"It seems to me you're not in any position to tell me what to do," the gunman snapped. "My pardner and I are in a hurry and our horses are done in, even more so than yours. You try and stop us from borrowin' them and you'll get a bellyful of lead for your trouble."

"I reckon you win, Mister," Jim shrugged, then pointedly added, "for now. But you two hombres had better watch your backs, because we'll be comin' after you. Bet a hat on it."

"That would be really stupid on your part," the horse thief replied as he reached for Sam's reins and lifted them from the rail. His attention fully on Jim, he failed to notice Blawcyzk's gelding pinning back his ears in warning. As the thief lifted his foot to the stirrup, Sam danced sideways and nipped wickedly at the gunman's shoulder, ripping his shirt as he just missed the flesh.

The outlaw viciously yanked down on Jim's paint's bit and quirted the gelding across his neck with the reins. His gun still aimed at the Ranger, he managed to pull himself onto Sam's back. The horse instantly exploded in a frenzy of bucking, crowhopping sideways and slamming the horse thief's leg into the rail. Sam spun, reversing direction, and the renegade was tossed from his back to slide face-first in the dirt.

With an oath, the gunman grabbed for the Colt he'd dropped as he hit the ground. Forgetting about Jim, he cursed at Sam, screaming oaths before he shouted, "I'll teach you a lesson you won't forget, you blasted spotted devil." He leveled his pistol at Sam's chest as the paint reared high, whinnying in fury.

"Drop that gun now!" Jim ordered, his Colt leaping into his hand.

"Why, you son of a ...!" the gunman snarled, whipping his gun around. Before he could pull his trigger Jim fired twice. The outlaw grunted in surprise and pain as both bullets took him in his stomach. His gun fell from his hand as he clutched at his middle and jackknifed slowly to the dirt. Sam brought his front hooves down square in the middle of the dying outlaw's back.

"Stop, Sam, he's had enough," Jim ordered. Still snorting in anger, Sam trotted up to Jim to nuzzle his shoulder.

Smoky's assailant had taken his gun off the Ranger when Sam had thrown his partner. He realized his mistake too late as Smoky dove at him, wrapping his arms around him and driving him against Soot's ribs. Smoky slammed a powerful right to the gunman's jaw, then sank a left deep into his belly. All air driven from his lungs, the outlaw dropped his gun as he folded into another right to his chin. His head snapped back from the force of the blow. As he started to sag, Smoky smashed a punch to the back of his neck and he crumpled to his face.

"All right you, get up!" Smoky ordered, grabbing the gunman by his shoulder and pulling him to his feet.

"Don't. Don't hit me again, Mister," the outlaw gasped. "I've had enough. Oww. My head." He reached for the back of his head as if to rub the bruise Smoky's punch had raised on his neck, then without warning pulled out a knife hanging in a neck sheath. Smoky jumped back as the knife was brought around in a vicious arc, ripping a slash across his shirt and barely missing sinking deep into his stomach. Blood trickled from a shallow gash the sharp pointed Bowie sliced along his upper abdomen.

As his assailant pulled back the knife for another thrust, Smoky jerked his Colt from its holster and fired once, the bullet striking the outlaw just under his left shirt pocket. He spun from the lead's impact and staggered up against Soot's side, then as the horse shied toppled under the steeldust's belly. Whickering nervously, Soot stepped aside, eyes rolling apprehensively as he eyed the dead gunman.

"What the devil's all the commotion about?", Jack Swanson, the trading post's owner, demanded as he stepped onto the sagging front porch. He held an old sawed-off Greener at the ready and leveled it at the two men still standing in the shadows. Swanson was a burly, bearded individual in his late forties, with a good sized paunch hanging over his belt. "Step over here into the light so I can get a look at you two hombres. Don't try anything funny. I can't miss with this scattergun at this range, and Zeb here's got his Sharps ready to blow a hole clean through you." He nodded at the buffalo hunter, who held a single shot .50 caliber rifle across his chest.

"Take it easy, Swanson," Jim softly answered. "Don't get nervous with that trigger finger of yours. This is the Texas Rangers."

"Lieutenant Blawcyzk?!" Swanson exclaimed as he recognized Jim's voice. He lowered his shotgun as he continued, "I should have known it was you when I heard that ruckus. And I'll bet that good for nothing Smoky McCue's ridin' with you as always. So what happened out here?"

"You've got us pegged, Jack," Jim admitted with a chuckle as he stepped into the lantern light. "It's me and Smoky, all right. A couple of hombres made the mistake of trying to steal our broncs. Bring that light down here so we can get a look at them, will you?"

"Sure," Swanson replied, lifting the lantern from the nail where it hung and descending from the porch.

Jim and Smoky rolled the lifeless outlaws onto their backs and dragged them over to where Swanson and Zeb waited.

"Do you recognize either of these hombres?" the trading post owner questioned as he shone the light on the dead men's faces.

Jim and Smoky studied the two bodies for a moment before Jim carefully stated, "I believe I do. What about you, Smoke?"

"I'm pretty certain the one you downed is Jack Doakes," Smoky replied, "which means the other hombre is his pardner, Ed Hills. They're a couple of the worst horse thieves and cattle rustlers to ever work this part of Texas. Maybe we'd better check their descriptions in the Fugitive List to make sure." The Fugitive List was a loosely bound book all Rangers carried, containing the names and descriptions of all known outlaws being sought in the state.

"We don't have to, unless you want to double-check on Hills," Jim replied. "I dealt with Doakes a few years back, and that's definitely him lyin' there with my bullets in his guts." Jim shook his head in disgust. "What a waste. If those hombres had listened they'd still be alive right now."

"And headed for a jail cell or hang rope," Smoky pointed out. "Besides which you warned them not to try stealing our horses, Jim. It's not your fault they didn't listen. And better it's them lyin' there full of lead rather than us. Plus at least there are two more men we can scratch off the Fugitive List."

"Your pardner's right," Zeb agreed, then glanced at Sam, who was still nuzzling at Jim's shoulder, along with taking an occasional playful nip at his rider's ear. "I never would guess that's the same cayuse who was ready to tear that hombre's head from his shoulders. He sure exploded when that jasper tried to mount him."

"Sam's pretty much a one man horse," Jim explained, as he patted the paint's neck. "I got him from a person who'd abused him for quite a while. It took him a long while to really trust me, but we've been together for quite a few years now. He only lets me or my son Charlie ride him." Jim chuckled as he added, "Well, and Sam and my wife kind of tolerate each other, which makes for some interesting moments around my place."

"I'd say for certain he saved your hide tonight, Ranger," Zeb replied.

"He's done that more than once," Jim answered. As Swanson shifted the lantern slightly and its light spilled on McCue, for the first time Blawcyzk noticed Smoky's ripped shirt and the blood slowly darkening the garment.

"Smoke, you're hurt!" Jim exclaimed. "You'd better let me check that."

"It's just a shallow cut," Smoky replied. "Nothing that can't wait until after we get these renegades planted. Jack, if you have a couple of shovels we can borrow we'll tend to that task."

"Nothin' doin', Ranger." Swanson objected. "Zeb and I can take care of that chore in the morning. For tonight we'll just roll those bodies up in a couple of blankets and stash them behind the corrals. Like your pardner says, you need to have that wound checked. Head inside and let Mourning Dove take a look at you. She'll fix you right up."

"I've got to take care of my horse first," Smoky objected.

"Don't worry about your bronc," Swanson rejoined. "My son will take care of him for you." He turned to call inside the post.

"Matthew! Come out here! It's all right now."

In answer to Swanson's call a boy of twelve or thirteen emerged from inside. He had Swanson's ruddy complexion, but the straight black hair and deep brown eyes of his Kiowa mother. His eyes bulged slightly at the sight of the two dead outlaws.

"Yeah, dad?" he quietly said.

"Take Ranger McCue's steeldust to the corral, rub him down really good, then feed and water him."

"Sure, dad," Matthew readily agreed. "How about the other Ranger's horse? Shall I take care of him too?"

"I think the Lieutenant would agree he should take care of his own horse," Swanson laughed.

"But I do appreciate the offer, son. Thanks," Jim broke in. "Smoky, that's settled. You get yourself patched up while the rest of us finish things up out here."

"I reckon you're not giving me much choice," Smoky grumbled.

"No, I'm not," Jim replied, "So do I have to make this a direct order?"

"You win," Smoky conceded, "Besides, that gives me first crack at Mourning Dove's stew."

Jim laughed heartily. "I should have known. It's always the food with you, Smoke."

"Not true," Smoky objected. "It's the food, the liquor, and the women."

As Smoky headed inside, Jim and Matthew headed for the corral with the Rangers' horses. Swanson and Zeb went with them, heading for the leanto to find blankets to cover the outlaws' bodies.

"Ranger, I didn't have a chance to introduce myself proper-like before the fireworks started," Zeb stated, "I'm Zebediah Butler at your service. And I want to apologize for not lending you and your pardner a hand quick enough when those renegades jumped you. They came out of the shadows so fast I didn't realize what was happenin' until they had their guns on you. My rifle was inside the store, so I tried to sneak in and retrieve it without their noticing. By the time I got my Sharps and made it back outside things were already pretty much over."

"I guess you need my name too," Jim replied, "It's Jim. Jim Blawcyzk. My pard's is Smoky McCue. And there's no apology necessary. Those hombres were real slick. I never guessed myself they were there until it was too late. Smoky and our horses missed them too."

"I should have realized those two were up to no good," Swanson added, "They rode up about an hour or so ago, ate real fast and had a couple of drinks. Said they had to keep movin' to catch up with some friends over Jacksboro way. They wanted to buy fresh horses from me, but I've only got that old mare of mine and my wagon horse. When I couldn't sell them any mounts, then they told me they'd stay overnight and let their horses rest. They paid me for bunks for themselves and board for their horses. I never guessed they'd lie in wait to drygulch somebody." Swanson chuckled as he concluded, "They sure picked on the wrong fellas when they tried to steal a couple of Texas Rangers' horses."

"I'd sure say so," Zeb agreed. He eyed Jim narrowly. "You said your name is Blaw ... Blaw ... Blaw *what*?"

"It's BLUH-zhick," Jim helped with a grin, used to people stumbling over his Polish surname. "Or you can do like Jack here, who insists on calling me Lieutenant. Most folks just call me Jim, though. It's a lot easier."

"You can say that again," Zeb laughed, as he opened the corral gate so the horses could be led inside.

Once the horses were inside and tied to the fence, Jim told Swanson, "Jack, I've got to send a letter to Austin and let Headquarters know

Doakes and Hill are dead. If you'll make up a bill for buryin' them, I'll send it along too."

""There's no need for that," Swanson replied. "I'm always glad to help out the Rangers. Besides," he nodded at two geldings, a blaze faced blue roan and a stocking footed bay which were wearily munching hay in a far corner of the corral, "I figure I've received two halfway decent horses and some ridin' gear in compensation for my trouble."

"That's certainly fair enough," Jim agreed. His blue eyes seemed like chips of ice as he studied the outlaws' worn out mounts. The exhausted animals were still coated with dried sweat and dirt. If there was one thing that could drive Jim to an almost unreasoning fury, it was someone abusing an animal.

"Jack, it looks like those two broncs need some tending to," he coldly stated. "Once Sam and Soot are settled in I'm going to rub them down too. I'm also going to check those renegades' gear before I head inside. Let Smoky know I'll be along shortly."

"If I know your McCue, with my wife and daughters fussing over him your pardner's already forgotten you're out here, Lieutenant," Swanson chortled.

"You're most likely right at that," Jim grinned, as he lifted the saddle from Sam's back. Before Matt removed Soot's saddle, Jim dug in Smoky's saddlebags to retrieve a spare shirt, which he handed to Swanson.

"You'd better take this with you for my pardner," Jim requested, "That shirt Smoky was wearing sure isn't much good now."

"I'll do that," Swanson promised as he took the shirt. "Zeb," he added to the buffalo hunter, "Those old blankets should be in the back corner of the leanto. Let's get those bodies covered and put away. Matt, make sure you do a thorough job of grooming Ranger McCue's horse."

"I will, Dad," Matt assured him.

"Jack, if you don't mind my borrowing your boy for a few minutes longer, I could use a hand with those other two horses," Jim requested.

"That's not a problem at all," Swanson agreed. "I'll see you inside in a bit."

While Swanson and Zeb removed the bodies of the outlaws to behind the leanto, Jim and Matt fed and groomed the Rangers' horses, then rubbed down the blue roan and bay. That done, Matt headed back inside, while Jim went through the contents of the dead men's saddlebags, which were hanging from the fence along with the rest of their gear. Except for a scrap of paper with Jack Doakes name scrawled across it, the *alforjas* contained no information of use to the Ranger. Finally the dead-tired lawman was ready to have his meal and get a good night's sleep.

"I'll see you in the mornin', Sam," he told his paint as he gave the horse a last peppermint and stroked his velvety muzzle. "Rest up, since we've still got a lot of miles to put behind us." Jim glanced up at the sky at the sound of a distant rumble of thunder, to see lightning flickering on the western horizon. "You might want to get under that leanto, pard," he told the gelding, "It looks like it's fixing to blow pretty good." As Sam nuzzled his shoulder, Jim then slapped him fondly on the neck, telling the mount, "G'night, bud." Sam responded with a soft whicker, then went back to munching his hay.

Jim headed inside and passed through the main room with its mounds of haphazardly stacked merchandise to find his partner smoking a quirly and stretched out on his back on a well-worn sofa in the good-sized combination dining and bar room. McCue's shirt and boots were off, and a foul smelling poultice had been plastered over the knife slash across his stomach. Mourning Dove, Swanson's Kiowa wife, was spoon-feeding Smoky from a bowl of hearty beef stew, while two dark-haired young women, in their late teens or early twenties, hovered over the wounded Ranger. A third young woman, with the same dark hair and eyes as her sisters, was at the cast-iron stove, placing Smoky's ripped, blood-stained shirt in a pot of hot soapy water. That shirt would be washed, mended, and returned to McCue before the Rangers left. Swanson was behind the bar, his head wreathed in clouds of smoke from the pipe clamped tightly between his teeth, while Zeb was at the mahogany nursing a beer.

"I hope you're comfortable, Smoke," Jim dryly remarked.

"I'm managing," Smoky replied with a grin, "Cherry, Young Fawn, and Natalie are taking good care of me. And of course Mourning Dove is patching me up just fine."

"Of course," Jim chuckled in reply.

"Ranger McCue is a good patient," Mourning Dove quietly said, "And his appetite for my stew makes my heart happy."

"I'm glad he's good for something," Jim laughed. "And if it's not too much trouble I could go for some of that good stew myself."

"It's no trouble, Lieutenant," Mourning Dove answered. "Cherry," she ordered the girl at the stove. "Please fill a bowl for the Ranger."

"Certainly, Mother," Cherry replied, smiling as she gazed at Blawcyzk. "I'd assume you would like some bread and butter to go along with it, Lieutenant. And coffee, beer, or whiskey?"

"I would indeed," Jim replied as he took a seat at the long table in the center of the room, where Matthew was already working on his second helping of stew. The Ranger's blue eyes reflected the smile Cherry's dark ones held. "And I'll have coffee, as long as it's strong and black."

"Cherry, you must have forgotten Lieutenant Blawcyzk doesn't drink anything containing alcohol," Swanson spoke up from behind the bar. "Lieutenant, I'll have a couple of cold sarsaparillas for you whenever you want."

"I reckon I'll wait until Smoke's ready for his whiskey," Jim replied.

"His wound will be bandaged by the time you are finished with your meal, so he will be able to join you," Mourning Dove promised.

"That's fine. Smoke and I are both grateful to you and your family," Jim answered as Cherry placed a deep bowl of stew, a plate of bread and butter, and a mug of coffee in front of him. He fell silent while he dug into the meal.

"Storm comin'." A few minutes later Jim glanced up at the flicker of lighting through the room's single grimy window. "It sure seems like we're in for a real gullywasher," he offhandedly remarked, as thunder rumbled in the distance and a cool breeze came through the open back door.

"I guess I'd better shut that door, even though it'll get mighty stuffy in here," Swanson grumbled. He stepped from behind the bar and pulled the door closed.

"We can use the rain," Zeb observed, "It's been awful dry in these parts. Worst I've seen it in years. Mebbe I'll have better travelin' when I head north to meet my partners in a few days. With luck this storm'll fill up a few of the waterholes and green up the grass some."

"Boy howdy, you're sure right about that," Swanson agreed. "Parson's Creek is runnin' less than half full."

"As long as it blows itself out before morning so it doesn't slow me and Smoky up," Jim noted. "We need to make the Panhandle as quickly as possible."

"You're headed for the Panhandle?" Swanson asked.

"That's right," Jim answered. "I was gonna ask you this while we were havin' our drinks later, but as long as you've brought it up … Jack, have you heard anything about a bunch maybe dressed like cavalry soldiers doing a whole lot of robbin' and killin' up that way?"

"Soldiers?" Swanson echoed. The trading post owner stroked his thick beard thoughtfully before he reluctantly replied. "I've heard a few stories about a bunch like that. I can't tell you much more than that, however. They've been operating much further north, or so I understand. But they're a pretty mean outfit, from what I hear tell."

"And you hear everythin' that goes on in north Texas, Jack." Smoky retorted as he sat up. The wounded Ranger now had a clean white bandage wrapped around his middle. "Don't try and keep anything from us."

"I tell you Rangers everythin' I find out," Swanson protested.

"Don't bother Jack with your questions," Zeb spoke up. "My pards and I've been huntin' buffalo up that way. We've heard all about those hombres. They're dressed like Yankee soldier boys, all right. In fact, I'd be willin' to bet a whole season's worth of hides they really are soldiers."

"Do you know that for certain?" Jim questioned. "There was only one witness who mentioned anything about the Army, from the reports Ranger Headquarters received."

"Mebbe when you left Austin," Zeb explained, "but those renegades have been busy since. Six days ago, they hit a party of buffalo hunters and stole three wagonloads of hides. Most of those hunters were friends of mine," he bitterly spat.

"But what makes you think it was the same bunch?" Jim pressed, "And how do you know they were in soldier's garb?"

"Because one of 'em left his hat behind," Zeb explained. "When me and my pards came upon what those hombres had left of our compadres we found Tate Hanson with that hat clutched in his hands. Tate was a real tough old hombre, and he wasn't quite dead when we found him, despite the three bullets in his guts. Before he cashed in, Tate managed to choke out it was a bunch of soldiers who'd killed him and his pards."

"Or men masquerading as soldiers," Smoky pointed out.

"You could be right," Zeb conceded. "Either way, you're lookin' for some *muy malo hombres,* Ranger."

"Tell us where this happened, Zeb," Jim demanded. "At least it might give us a start on where to look for those renegades."

"It was about ten or twelve miles northwest of that little settlement folks call Jayton," the buffalo hunter explained, "but I'm sure those devils are long gone by now."

"But it does give us an idea which way to head come morning," Jim answered.

"That is if we can ride out at all," Smoky rejoined, as the room was illuminated by an almost blinding flash of lightning and thunder rattled the window, followed immediately by the spattering of raindrops. "We'd best get our bedrolls before the downpour begins."

"Don't worry about your blankets," Swanson urged. "I've got plenty of those stacked up on the back counter. I'll just have Matthew grab you a couple and you can throw 'em down on the floor right in here. Son, get the Rangers those blankets."

"Right away, Dad," Matthew complied, disappearing into the main merchandise room. He returned a few moments later carrying an armful of woolen blankets. By the time the blankets were spread on the floor, the storm had commenced in full fury. Wind-driven rain lashed the building, accompanied by vivid lightning and deafening claps of thunder.

"Lieutenant, I know you wanted to hit the sack early, but even you can't sleep through this racket," Swanson noted as Jim finished his meal. "How about a few hands of poker before you turn in? And I'll dig out those sarsaparillas for you."

"That doesn't sound like a half-bad idea," Jim grinned. "I'll be more'n happy to take some of your cash."

"And I'll take Jack's cash from you, pard," Smoky chuckled as he padded stocking-footed for the card table in the back corner.

"Before you start playing, Ranger, you had best finish dressing before you catch a chill," Mourning Dove ordered McCue, as she handed him his spare shirt and freshly polished boots. "And I will have your other shirt washed and mended for you by morning."

"I reckon you're right," Smoky agreed, shrugging into the shirt and tugging on the boots. "Now, Jack, how about some of your finest red-eye?"

"Comin' right up," Swanson smiled, as he took a bottle and three glasses from behind the bar. Picking up two bottles of pop from under the counter, he joined the two Rangers and Zeb at the baize-covered table. After filling the glasses and opening a sarsaparilla for Jim, he unwrapped a new deck of cards.

"Anything particular you feel like playing?" Swanson queried as he removed the jokers and shuffled the cards.

"Five card stud's fine with me," Jim replied.

"All right. Any objections?" Swanson asked. When Smoky and Zeb answered in the negative, he began tossing cards around the table.

❧   ❧   ❧

The four men had been playing for just over an hour when the front door slammed open and three cowhands in water-dripping slickers stepped into the room. They pulled off the coats and hung them from a wall peg, then slapped their soaked Stetsons against their legs to drive water from the brims.

"Howdy, Jack," one of the men called out. "I sure hope you've got some whiskey handy. We're drenched, and could really use some red-eye to warm up."

"The Norman brothers!" Swanson exclaimed as he pushed back from the table. "Howdy yourselves, boys! What in blue blazes brings you two good-for-nothings out on a night like this? And who's that hombre with you?"

"This is our new foreman, Tom Treloar," the elder of the brothers answered. "We're on our way back from a stock-buyin' trip over San Angelo way. We didn't find any good cows like we'd hoped, but we did hire on Tom here. We'd planned to make it home by morning, but we got caught out in this storm. We never expected it to blow up so fast. In fact we nearly missed your place. Didn't see it until we were just about on top of it. Our horses are about done in, so we turned 'em loose in your corral and tossed some hay to them. Figured you wouldn't mind none."

"Well, just make yourselves to home," Swanson invited, then continued, "These gents are Jim Blawcyzk and Smoky McCue. They're Rangers. The other hombre is Zeb Butler."

"Pleased to meet you," Norman spoke as the trio headed for the bar. "I reckon we should furnish our handles. I'm Patrick Norman, and this ugly lookin' hombre here is my kid brother, Ronny. You've already gotten Tom's name."

"Same here," Jim answered, eyeing the newcomers narrowly. If he hadn't been told, Jim never would have guessed two of the men were brothers, as they looked alike not at all. Patrick Norman was stocky and fair, with pale eyes and tow hair so bleached by the Texas sun it was the color of straw, his eyebrows so light they were hardly visible. His skin, so fair it was evidently incapable of tanning, was reddened by exposure to sun and wind. His younger brother Ronny was slightly less stocky, but had dark brown hair and eyes, with a complexion to match.

As Jim studied the men, Mourning Dove emerged from the kitchen.

"Hey! You squaw!" Treloar instantly demanded. "I want grub. Chuck. Food. Now. You comprende?"

"I assume you want some victuals for your evening repast," Mourning Dove mildly replied, her studied politeness in stark contrast to Treloar's rude command. Treloar flushed deep red as the other occupants of the room burst into laughter.

"Tom," Patrick Norman explained once his guffaws had subsided, "Mourning Dove speaks English far better than you. In fact, she probably speaks it better'n anyone else in this room."

"That's right," Swanson spoke up. "My wife here was captured by white traders as a child and she was educated at a convent school in St. Louis. She speaks English, Spanish, and French equally well, and of course her native Kiowa. In fact, she even knows a smattering of Hebrew."

"Then I reckon I owe you an apology, ma'am," Treloar said. "I've never come across an educated Indian before. I've only dealt with a few border-jumpin' Comanches and Apaches in my time. I guess I won't be gettin' that grub."

"I'll accept your apology," Mourning Dove answered, "As long as you remember the lesson you just learned."

"I surely will," Treloar promised. "Guess I really put my foot in my mouth."

"And I'm sure it didn't taste as good as my beef stew will," Mourning Dove smiled mischievously as she slid a bowlful in front of the cowboy, as well as the two Norman brothers. "Enjoy."

"Thank you, ma'am. I sure will," Treloar answered as he dug hungrily into the stew.

Jim questioned the Normans as they ate, his casual manner carefully calculated to avoid raising any suspicions on their part.

"Where're you boys from?" was his first query.

"Our spread's the Rockin' N Ranch. It's still about a day's ride northeast of here," Ronny explained while he shoved another spoonful of stew in his mouth. "With the full moon we'd figured on ridin' all night to make it home, but this storm sure ruined our plans, worse luck."

"It slowed us down some too," Jim answered. "We just beat it here. How long have you fellas been gone from home?"

"The better part of a month," Patrick answered, "And we're sure eager to get back. We left some good hands in charge, but there's always rustlers to contend with, it seems. That's why we hired Tom here as our new foreman. Our last one, Buzz Coltrain, got shot up real bad by a band of cattle rustlers. He's gonna be laid up for a long time, and he'll probably never ride a bronc again."

"Then you wouldn't know anything about a bunch dressed as U.S. cavalry soldiers raising a whole mess of Cain up north of here, robbin' stages and such, murderin' their victims so there's no witnesses left alive," Jim continued.

"No," Ronny answered. "I've gotta say that's news to us … not good news, I might add. There's already enough trouble in this territory, what with rustlers and outlaws, not to mention reservation jumpin' Indians."

"Are you Rangers headed up north to try and put a stop to some of that trouble?" Patrick broke in.

"That's what we're aimin' to do," Jim answered.

"If that's the case, why don't you ride along with us as far as our spread?" Patrick invited. "Like my brother said, it's about a day's ride from here, so we can put you up for the night then you can head on from there. We've got a couple of spare bunks and Win Chow, our cook, puts out some pretty decent grub."

"You mean chow," Jim grinned, unable to resist the obvious bad joke.

"I reckon you're right at that," Patrick conceded with a chuckle. "Anyway, the invitation's open if you'd like to take advantage of it."

Jim thought carefully before replying, "I dunno. We'll be traveling hard and fast. We don't have the time to dawdle."

"We're in a hurry too, Lieutenant," Patrick answered. "We've been away from our spread way too long, so we're just as anxious to cover ground as you are."

"What do you say, Smoke?" Jim asked his partner.

"We could do worse, I guess," Smoky replied, as he took a puff of his cigarette. "As long as the storm blows itself out by mornin', I reckon we might as well ride along with these fellas. I wouldn't mind spending a night in a bed rather than on the hard ground."

"We won't be putting you out?" Jim asked the brothers.

"Not at all," Ronny replied. "We'd be glad to have you."

"I guess we'll head out with you boys then," Jim answered, adding as a warning, "But we do ride out at sunup."

"That's not a problem," Patrick responded. "Since we'll want to get an early start ourselves, we'll be hittin' our blankets as soon as we finish eating. So that's settled. You'll spend tomorrow night at the Rocking N."

"If we're ridin' out at sunup, then we'd better call it a night too, Jim," Smoky observed. "How about we quit after we finish this last hand?"

"That makes sense," Jim agreed.

"I'm going to close down early anyway," Swanson added. "There won't be any more travelers out in this storm. Pat, like I told the Rangers, if you want I'll have Matthew get some blankets from the store for y'all and you can bed down right here."

"That's certainly a generous offer," Patrick agreed.

"Fine. Matthew, get those blankets," Swanson ordered.

Less than thirty minutes later, the lights of the trading post, except for one dimly burning wall lamp, were extinguished. The Swanson family retired to their quarters, while their guests rolled in blankets on the barroom floor to settle in for the night.

CHAPTER 6

One reason Jim had been hesitant to ride along with the Norman brothers and their foreman was his concern their horses would be unable to keep up with Sam and Soot. However his fears had proven unfounded, as all three of the Rocking N men were well-mounted, Patrick on a blocky palomino mustang, Ronald on a chunky strawberry roan, and Tom on a rangy blaze-faced chestnut. With good horses eager to travel under them, the group made better time than they'd hoped and now, about an hour before sunset, were briefly resting the horses atop a low rise overlooking the Rocking N Ranch. The spread was nestled in a small valley, its buildings and corrals carefully placed for shelter from the almost ceaseless north Texas winds. The setting sun painted the rough-hewn log buildings with a warm glow. On the front porch of the main house a man sat in a rocker, his legs covered by a woolen blanket.

"That certainly is a nice-lookin' place you boys have there," Smoky observed as he rolled and lit a quirly.

"We put a lot of hard work into the Rocking N," Patrick replied. "But it's been worth it. In another year it'll be fixed up enough so I'll finally be able to bring my gal down here from Pennsylvania and marry her."

"That's Buzz Coltrain on the porch," Ronny added. "Sure is good to see him on the mend." He glanced over at Treloar. "Tom, do you like what you see?"

"The spread looks mighty good to me so far," Treloar replied, "And I'm just grateful for the chance to hang my hat in one place for a spell. I only hope the men will accept me, bein' as I'm a newcomer and will be takin' Buzz's place."

"You don't have to worry about that," Patrick assured the new hand, "You'll do just fine."

"If you hombres are just about through jawin', let's get moving," Jim impatiently urged. "Smoke and I have got to get another early start tomorrow."

"Right you are, Lieutenant," Patrick grinned, sketching a rough salute in jest, "Let's go!" He dug his spurs into his mustang's ribs, sending the mount leaping forward, the others strung out behind as they galloped down the hill.

By the time they pounded through the gate and into the ranch yard, Blawcyzk's paint had pulled ahead by several lengths. From the porch, Buzz Coltrain gazed at the Ranger intently as he pulled Sam to a plunging halt. A moment later, as the rest of the group reined to a halt in front of the house, a Chinese man wearing a clean white apron over his clothes emerged onto the porch to stand alongside Coltrain. Attracted by the commotion, two youthful cowboys came from the bunkhouse to join the rest.

"That sure is some horse you've got there, Lieutenant," Patrick praised with frank admiration as his mustang slid to a stop, "Still able to run like that after puttin' all those miles behind him."

"Thanks," Jim replied, "I'm pretty fond of him."

Patrick turned his attention to the man in the rocker. "Howdy, Buzz. We're home."

"I can see that. I may be crippled up, but I'm not yet blind," Coltrain softly drawled, the twinkle in his deep gray eyes taking any sting out of his words, "And you sure seemed in an all-fired hurry to get here, the way you ran those horses down that hill. And who the devil are all these hombres you dragged along with you?"

"You're as ornery as ever, Buzz," Patrick chuckled. "This here gentleman on the big paint is Ranger Lieutenant Jim Blawcyzk. That's his pardner Smoky McCue on the steeldust. They'll be spendin' the night with us. The other one is Tom Treloar. We've hired him on as acting foreman until you're well enough to work again. After that, Tom will stay on as *segundo*, as long as you and he hit it off."

"You mean if I can work again," Coltrain gently corrected his boss. "There's no use kiddin' ourselves. That slug I took in my hip has pretty well ended my ridin' days. Tom, welcome to the Rocking N. I'm sure you'll work out just dandy."

"Thanks," Treloar quietly replied as he shook Coltrain's hand, "And I'll be counting on you to help me learn the routine around here."

"I'll do just that," Coltrain answered, "At least I'll be doin' something useful again." He paused before turning his attention to the two Rangers. "Howdy to you boys too. In case you haven't already figured it out, I'm Buzz Coltrain. This hombre behind me is Win Chow, the ranch cook. Don't let his looks fool you. He can cook American and Texan as good as anyone. And these other two are Brad Turley and Wes Adams." The two cowpunchers nodded their greetings to the Rangers.

"I guess I'll have to set five more places for supper," Win Chow grunted, his expression unchanging. "Supper will be on the table in an hour. Don't be late or you'll go hungry tonight." He fixed the Normans with an icy stare. "That also goes for you, boss men."

"He means it, too," Ronny chuckled. "So if we want our chuck tonight we'd best get these horses cared for and ourselves washed up. Rangers, there's a couple of empty stalls for your horses, or if you prefer you can just turn them out in the corral."

"I think our broncs will appreciate a stall for the night," Jim replied. "Just show us where to put them."

"Sure, Lieutenant. We'll have them settled in right quick." Patrick answered as he turned his palomino toward the barn. "Right this way."

The tired horses were soon rubbed down and turned into stalls with a full measure of grain and hay, Sam as usual getting his peppermint from Jim. Once that was done, the men washed up at the bench in back of the barn, then headed for the house.

"You are two minutes late," Win Chow scolded, "I was giving you one more minute then your supper was going to feed the hogs."

"Win Chow hates to have his grub get cold waitin' on anyone," Patrick explained with a chuckle, as they took their seats at a long board table and began to dig into the meal. The cook had prepared thick beef-steaks, accompanied by peas, carrots, and, instead of the usual fried potatoes, rice.

"First time I've eaten rice in a coon's age," Smoky observed as he heaped his plate high with the starchy white grain. "Last time was way over in east Texas, close to the Louisiana border. Have to say I haven't missed it all that much."

"Rice is very good for you," Win Chow retorted. "Much healthier than potatoes. You eat Ranger, or no apple pie and coffee."

"I'm eating it, I'm eating," Smoky hastily rejoined. "It's real good too, Win Chow." As on most ranches, when it came to mealtime the cook ruled with an iron hand. Win Chow was no exception.

The conversation around the supper table was the usual ranch discussion of cattle prices, weather, and rustlers, along with the Normans and their hands catching up on what had transpired while they were gone. Patrick noted to his satisfaction that Tom Treloar seemed to be accepted without question by Coltrain, Turley, and Adams. Once the meal was finished the men settled on the porch with cups of strong black coffee, several of them building and lighting quirlies.

"I've got the rest of the boys out combin' the back breaks along the river for some of the stock that wanders out that way," Coltrain explained in answer to Ronny's inquiry as to what the rest of the Rocking N hands were doing. "They've already gathered quite a few cows, and are holding 'em in that box canyon north of the breaks. We should have a nice bunch ready to ship by the time they're finished."

"That's good thinkin'," Ronny answered, then told Treloar, "Tom, I reckon we should ride out there in the morning and introduce you to the rest of the boys."

"That sounds right to me," Treloar agreed, as he tipped back in his chair to roll and light a cigarette. "I just hope I can do as good a job as I hear Buzz has done for you fellas."

"You'll do all right," Coltrain assured him. "And a young fella like yourself might even come up with some new ideas."

"Well, we'll see," Tom answered. "In the meantime I'd like to get some shut-eye."

"I think we're all ready for that," Patrick agreed. He turned to the Rangers. "Lieutenant, Corporal, you can take your pick of the empty beds in the bunkhouse. We'll see you first thing in the morning."

"Sure thing," Jim responded. "And thanks again for your hospitality."

"Don't mention it," Patrick replied. "We're glad to have you."

"We still appreciate the hot meal and beds," Jim answered. "Good night. See you at breakfast."

Blawcyzk, McCue, Treloar, Turley, and Adams were quickly undressed and stretched out on their mattresses in the airy Rocking N bunkhouse. Brad Turley proved exceedingly garrulous, talking virtually nonstop as they got ready for bed, still conversing as they settled under their blankets. When his conversation turned to the subject of yet another stagecoach robbery in the lower Panhandle, Jim and Smoky's interest was instantly piqued.

"I know you two are headed up that way to try and find whoever's behind all the robbin' and killin' up there," Turley continued without pause before they could even question him. "All I know is that it's gotta be a mighty mean bunch pulling off those holdups. They don't care who they kill, even women and kids, as long as they don't leave any witnesses."

"Brad, have you heard anything about some cavalry being involved?" Jim questioned.

"I've heard that story, sure," Turley replied. "Anyone who knows about the robberies does. That's all it is, though … a story. It could be anyone … even some Rangers."

"Easy, Smoke," Jim cautioned, as his partner was ready to leap out of bed and attack the Rocking N cowboy for his observation. "If we didn't know for a fact there aren't any Rangers in the territory besides us right now, we'd have to consider that possibility. Not that it makes your remark any easier to swallow, Turley!" Jim snapped.

"No offense meant, Lieutenant," Turley quietly replied. "I was just making the point no one has any idea where to look for these renegades, or who they are."

"I think you've said more than enough for one night, Brad," Wes Adams spoke up sleepily from his bunk. "We're all tired. It's high time to get to sleep."

"Your pardner's got the right idea," Smoky agreed as he rolled onto his stomach. "Good night!"

Turley was still talking softly as Jim said his evening prayers. Even as the rest of the men drifted off to sleep, Turley's voice still continued ringing in their ears.

🍁   🍁   🍁

Several hours later, the men were roused from their sleep by a horse galloping into the yard and the urgent shouts of a frantic rider. Instantly awake, they pulled on jeans and boots, then grabbed their pistols before racing out of the bunkhouse. Slumped over the neck of an exhausted sorrel gelding was a badly wounded cowboy, a splotch of crimson staining the back of his shirt. He slowly slipped off of his horse and thudded face-down to the dirt as the Norman brothers pounded down the porch steps.

"Toby!" Patrick exclaimed as he rolled the injured man onto his back, revealing a face of no more than seventeen or eighteen. "What the devil happened? Who shot you?"

"Rustlers!" the waddy gasped out. "They hit us just as most of the men were beddin' down. We were drygulched without any warning, and they had those cows runnin' before we even knew what was happening."

"What about the rest of the men, Toby?" Ronny anxiously asked.

"All ... all dead," Toby choked out. "I would've been too, if I hadn't played possum. Guess those rustlers figured I was done for with this bullet in my back. Reckon ... reckon ... they figured ... right."

"No, they didn't," Patrick assured the young cowboy. "You're gonna pull through." Win Chow and Buzz Coltrain had come onto the porch. "Win Chow, get Toby inside the house and tend to him. You're gonna have to dig the slug out of his back. Wes, help Win Chow get Toby onto my bed. Then get right back here."

"Right away, boss," Win Chow responded, as he came down the steps and slid his hands under the wounded man's shoulders, while Wes grasped Toby's ankles. "I'll fix him up, you'll see. Once that bullet is out, I've got herbs from my country that will pull any poisons from his blood. Toby boy will be just fine."

"You're goin' after those cussed cattle thieves and murderers, ain't you?" Coltrain asked.

"We sure are," Patrick answered, a deadly glint coming into his pale eyes as he watched Toby carried into the house. "Tom, Brad, get dressed and have your horses saddled in ten minutes. Fetch a couple of shovels too." He glanced over at Jim and Smoky. "Are you Rangers ridin' with us?"

"From what Buzz said at supper, your cattle were bein' held north of here," Jim replied, "That's on our way. We'll side you." Jim carefully avoided mentioning he and Smoky would ride with the Rocking N crew to hopefully not only capture the rustlers but also avoid the lynching which was certain to happen if the enraged cowmen caught up to the renegades without the law present.

"*Bueno*", Patrick replied as he glanced at the pale gray light of the false dawn streaking the eastern horizon. "It'll be light enough to see tracks real soon. And those rustlers won't be able to travel as fast as they'd like, pushin' that herd. With luck we'll catch up to 'em before sundown. Let's get to the horses."

"Sure wish I could ride with you," Coltrain wistfully remarked from where he stood, leaning against the porch rail to support his injured hip. "I'd teach those bushwhackin' sons a lesson they wouldn't soon forget."

"We'd feel better if you were sidin' us Buzz," Ronny responded. "But since that's not possible you'll be a big help by keepin' an eye on Toby along with Win Chow, and watching the place for us."

"I'll do just that," Coltrain reassured him, "And I'll grab some grub for you fellas while you saddle the horses. It'll be ready for you by the time you're done."

While Coltrain packed sacks of cold beef and leftover biscuits and Win Chow began to work on Toby, the rest of the men hurriedly finished dressing, then saddled their horses. Fifteen minutes later, seven men bent on justice trotted their mounts northward from the Rocking N.

CHAPTER 7

The sun was two hours above the eastern horizon when the men reached the site of the ambush. Four cowboys lay sprawled in various poses of death where they'd fallen to rustler bullets.

"We're gonna take the time to bury these men," Patrick needlessly ordered, his voice tight with emotion as he rolled one of the dead men onto his back. "Stace, we're gonna get the hombres who did this to you, I promise."

"And when we do we'll make 'em sorry they were ever born," Ronny added. "Let's get this done with so we can get back on their trail."

Wes and Brad took the shovels from their saddles and began to dig the first shallow grave. Within an hour the four slain Rocking N hands were laid in their final resting places, crude wooden crosses shoved into the ground at the head of each grave.

"Lord, take these good men home to rest in peace with You," Patrick intoned as he and the others stood with heads bowed and hats in hand. "And we ask Your guidance as we search for their killers. Amen."

"Amen." the rest of the group echoed.

Once they were back in their saddles Patrick turned to Blawcyzk.

"Lieutenant," he requested, "I'd appreciate it if you Rangers would take the lead. I imagine you and your pardner are far better trackers than any of us."

"That doesn't hardly matter," Jim responded as he leaned from his horse to study the obvious tracks left by the rustled herd. "A blind man could follow the trail these hombres left. I guess they figured they'd killed all of your men, and the missing cows wouldn't be discovered for quite some time. They're taking their time. Probably think that by the time anyone came after 'em, they'd be long gone. We're gonna prove 'em wrong. But before we go any further, I want to make one thing absolutely clear. There'll be no lynching of those rustlers once we catch up with them."

"I've got a rope just itchin' to stretch those murderin' cow thieves' necks," Ronny protested as he lifted his lariat from the saddle, "And there's plenty of cottonwoods along the creek bottoms we can use for a gallows."

"You heard what I said," Jim snapped. "We'll try to bring those men in alive for trial, if at all possible. I doubt they'll submit to arrest, so that means we'll have a fight on our hands, that's for certain. But I still intend to take them to jail. And if anyone tries to lynch those hombres he'll be the one facin' a rope. Bet a hat on it. Is that understood?"

"I reckon it is," Ronny grumbled. "But it still sticks in my craw."

"I know," Jim softly replied, "But lynchin' those men would make us no better than they are. Now let's get after 'em." He dug his bootheels into Sam's ribs, sending the big paint trotting ahead. Once the horses had warmed up, Jim pushed Sam into a ground-covering lope, with Smoky and the Rocking N crew trailing close behind.

❧   ❧   ❧

For better than an hour Jim and his companions kept up a brisk pace as they followed the trail of the stolen cattle, which led almost directly to the northeast. Finally, he pulled Sam to a halt alongside a shallow stream. Sam immediately dropped his nose to the clear water to drink, the other horses following suit.

"We're gonna take ten minutes to rest the horses, men," he announced, as he cocked his right leg comfortably across his saddlehorn.

"Seems to me we're taking it too slow, and those renegades are gettin' away from us," Treloar protested.

"There's no use in killin' our cayuses," Smoky pointed out, as he pulled tobacco and papers from his vest pocket and began to roll a quirly. "We do that, and those hombres will get away for sure."

"The Rangers are right, Tom," Ronny agreed. "We need these horses as ready to run as they can be."

"I stopped for another reason," Jim added, as he took a long pull on his canteen. "We've been gainin' steadily on those rustlers. And I'm fairly certain they'll do what most all cow thieves do. They'll hole up pretty soon, if they haven't done so already. They'll stay hunkered down until after sundown, then start movin' those cows again under the cover of dark. We sure don't want to ride up on them without realizing it. That'd be the perfect way to get bullets through our bellies before we even knew what hit us."

"Then what have you got in mind, Lieutenant?" Patrick questioned.

"You boys know this territory better than me or Smoke," Jim answered. "Can any of you think of any place where those cows could be bunched up, bedded down, and held without too much trouble, and where they most likely wouldn't be seen?"

"There's lots of canyons and river breaks all through these parts," Patrick answered. "One's pretty much as likely as another."

"Pat's right," Wes Adams agreed, as he bit a chaw off a plug of tobacco, "If we lose this trail, finding those rustlers'll be harder than finding a needle in a haystack."

"I think our best bet is to follow these tracks a while longer," Ronny advised. "Once we get a little further on maybe we can narrow down where they're headed."

"I've gotta agree with you," Brad Turley said, "We'll know more if we can get a little closer to those rustlers."

"Then that's what we'll do," Jim decided, "But if any of you comes up with an idea where these hombres are headed, let me know."

"We'll do just that," Patrick promised.

"Fine." Jim replied. "Smoky, once you and Tom finish your cigarettes, we'll get movin' again."

"Finished," Smoky answered, as he took one last drag on his quirly, then tossed the butt in the creek. He lifted his reins and sent Soot splashing across the stream.

Forty minutes later, Ronny reined his roan to a halt as he called out, "Hold it, Lieutenant. I think I've figured out where those rustlers are headed." The others reined in their horses and gathered around him.

"Where do you think they're goin'?" Jim asked.

"I could be wrong, but I've got a gut feelin' they're aimin' for Dawson's Draw," Ronny responded. "How about it, Patrick? What do you think?"

"I think you may well be right," Patrick agreed. "It'd make sense."

"Where's Dawson's Draw?" Smoky asked.

"It's another six miles north of here, more or less," Ronny explained. "We've used it on occasion when we were drivin' cows north. It's got decent water and grass, so it's real easy to keep a herd quiet in there. And it's a pretty deep arroyo, so unless you headed straight in there you could ride right on by without ever knowin' a herd of cattle was in that draw."

"Is there more than one way in and out of there?" Jim questioned.

"There's one main entrance," Patrick answered, "and it's fairly wide. There's also a trail out of the other end of the draw, but it's narrow and steep. It's plenty rocky, too. There's no way you can make a cow take that trail."

"How about a man on horseback?" Jim pressed. "Could he make it up that trail?"

"He could, but it'd be mighty tough," Patrick answered.

"I know what you're driving at, Lieutenant," Ronny broke in, "But we can't take the time to send a couple men to guard that back trail. Dawson's Draw is about seven miles long, so it'd take too long to get anyone around it. Plus a rider headin' down that trail'd make plenty of racket and kick up a lot of dust. That'd warn anyone in there he was comin'."

"Then we'll have to go straight in after them," Jim observed. "How's the cover in there once we get in? And it's pretty certain they'll have at least one man guarding the entrance. What are the chances we can spot him before he sees us?"

"I'd say we could get fairly close before they'd know we were in there," Patrick speculated. "There's lots of brush and plenty of good-sized loose rocks. As far as a guard, the most likely spot he'd be is on an outcropping about a quarter mile into the draw. We'd have to take care of him before we could get any further."

"What about waitin' until after dark?" Adams questioned. "That way it'd be easier to sneak up and get the drop on them before they spotted us."

"That's not a bad idea, but it'd also be easier for them to get past us," Jim explained, "and we'd have a hard time telling who was shootin' at who if any gunplay started. One of us might end up pluggin' one of his pards."

"Jim's right," Smoky said, adding, "And don't forget we're still not absolutely certain those rustlers are holed up in Dawson's Draw. If we wait until nightfall to go after them and they're not there, we'll have given them enough time to put so much distance between us that we'd probably never catch up to them."

"I guess you're right at that," Adams shrugged. "So how are we gonna pull this off?"

"We'll follow these tracks to the draw," Jim replied, "They should lead us right to our men if that's where they headed. We'll stop just outside the entrance and go in slow and easy in from there. If any of your broncs like to call out to other cayuses you'll have to tie a bandanna over their noses to muzzle 'em before we head in there so they don't give us away."

"What about the guard?" Treloar queried.

"I'm coming to that," Jim answered. "Except for you, Tom, all of you know that draw better than me or Smoky. Any of you think he might be able to get in there without being spotted, see if there is a guard posted, and if there is take care of him without him crying out and warning his compadres?"

"I think I can manage that," Ronny quickly spoke up. "There's good cover along the base of the right wall all the way to that outcrop. I should be able to see anyone up there before he spots me. And I can get behind him by climbing a crevice that runs up the side of the draw."

"*Bueno*", Jim answered, "But I want that man alive if at all possible. And I don't need to warn you if you're not careful and you're discovered, that guard'll warn his pardners and we'll have one heckuva fight on our hands."

"We're liable to have one anyway," Patrick pointed out.

"I'm afraid you're right," Jim agreed. "And that brings up something else. If any shooting starts, we need to make sure we stay between the herd and the draw's mouth. Those cows are sure to start runnin' at the first sound of gunfire, and we want to make sure they head for the back of the draw. That way, once they run up against that steep wall you fellas mentioned, they'll bunch back on themselves and start millin'. That should stop any stampede before it gets started, which'll save a lot of cattle, not to mention most likely our own hides. Any questions?"

"You seem to have everything covered, Lieutenant," Brad Turley answered, "Except how to keep from gettin' a slug through our guts."

"If I said I knew the answer to that, I'd be lying," Jim grimly chuckled. "Let's get movin'. If we push, we can make the draw in little more than an hour. We'll check our weapons just before we get there. C'mon Sam, let's go." He pushed the gelding into a long, mile eating gallop.

❦   ❦   ❦

"They went in there all right," Jim noted, as ninety minutes later he studied the dim trail which led into Dawson's Draw. The rustlers had not even attempted to hide the tracks of the stolen cattle, so confident they were of the theft not being discovered until pursuit was too late.

"Let's hope they're still in the draw," Patrick noted.

"They are," Jim answered. "There's no tracks comin' out."

"How many do you think we're up against?" Treloar asked.

"There's no way of telling," Jim replied, "The horses' hoofprints are mixed in with the cows', so they're pretty well obliterated."

"You can be sure it's a good-sized bunch though, to move this many cows this fast," Smoky observed. "I'd say about a dozen or so."

"We're about to find out in any event," Jim said. "Ronny, we'll take cover in that grove of post oaks until you scout out the situation for us. How long will it take you to get to that outcropping and back? You'll have to leave your horse here and go in on foot."

"It shouldn't take me more than a half hour," Ronny confidently replied. "Less if they didn't post a guard."

"Fine. We'll give you an hour, and if you haven't come back by then we'll come in after you."

"That's all very well, but if you hear any shots, come a-runnin'," Ronny replied, as he pulled off his boots and spurs, Stetson, and gunbelt.

"You can count on it," Patrick told him. "Be real careful, brother."

"Well, if I don't come back, you'll have the Rocking N all for yourself," Ronny ruefully laughed as he shoved his Colt into the waistband of his jeans. "Don't worry. I have no intention of gettin' my hide punctured. There. Guess I've taken off anything that might clink on the rocks and give me away. I'm ready."

"Good luck," Jim softly told him. "We'll see you in a bit."

"Count on it," Ronny replied, as he disappeared into the mouth of the draw.

The wait for Ronny's return seemed to take hours to his anxiously awaiting companions, whose nerves were already tight. While they waited they checked their guns, several times over. Not taking any chance of tipping off the rustlers, Jim wouldn't allow any smoking lest a whiff of tobacco smoke drift to the renegades' hideout. Not being able to puff on cigarettes only added to the tension for Smoky and the Rocking N hands. While the wait seemed endless, in fact it was only twenty minutes later when a dry twig sharply crackled. Several of the men jumped at the report, jerking around as their hands dropped to their guns, only to see Ronny grinning sheepishly as he emerged from the draw.

"You hombres a little jumpy?" he asked.

"That's a good way to get yourself shot, kid," Treloar grumbled.

"Sorry. I didn't see that branch lying there," Ronny apologized.

"Don't worry about that," Jim impatiently snapped. "What about the guard? Did they post one or not?"

"I've got good news, Lieutenant," Ronny replied as he picked up his gunbelt, hat, boots and spurs and quickly pulled them on. "They didn't. Guess they figured no one'd come after 'em, at least not until they were long gone. So what're we waitin' for? Let's go get 'em." He swung into the saddle of his strawberry roan.

"Fine," Jim replied. "Remember, we're gonna take those renegades alive if we possibly can. But if they put up a fight, once the shootin' starts shoot straight and fast. Let's mount up."

"I hope they do put up a fight," Patrick muttered. "I'd like nothing better than to put bullets through a few of those hombres' guts for what they did to our men."

"Unless I miss my guess, you'll have that chance right quick," Smoky answered. "You ready, Jim?"

"We're ready," Blawcyzk replied, as he eased Sam into the mouth of the draw.

More than six miles into the draw, Jim called a halt.

"I can smell wood smoke. We're closing in on them," he half-whispered. "Get your guns out. Remember, don't fire unless I give the word ... or they start shootin' first." Silently he slid the Winchester from its scabbard under his leg and laid it across the pommel of his saddle. Once the rest of the men had their weapons at the ready, Jim put Sam into a slow, almost silent walk.

Minutes later, the Rangers and Rocking N hands rounded a bend in the draw. Just beyond a shallow stream and a thin screen of brush were the rustlers, several of whom were sitting around a campfire. Beyond them was the stolen Rocking N herd, peacefully grazing the lush grass which grew almost to the back wall of the draw. Two of the rustlers were slowly circling the browsing cattle on horseback, keeping them bunched between the campfire and the draw's steep sides and preventing any strays from wandering back down the arroyo.

Jim lifted his Winchester to his shoulder, then as he and his partners emerged from their cover he called out sharply, "Texas Rangers! You're all under arrest! Keep your hands away from your guns, and raise them over your heads!"

For a moment, the rustlers were frozen, not believing their eyes at the sight of the lawmen. Then with a curse one of them grabbed for the pistol on his hip. He had the gun halfway leveled before Jim pulled the trigger of his rifle and put a bullet into the outlaw's chest. The rustler spun from the bullet's impact and fell face-first across the campfire.

The other cow thieves went for their guns, and as the Rangers and ranchmen returned fire two of them were dropped before they could pull triggers. Yet another went down when Treloar put a bullet through his throat. One of the rustlers on horseback pulled out his Winchester and fired a hasty shot, his bullet tearing a hole through Ronny's left arm. The younger Norman's return shot ripped into the renegade's stomach, jackknifing him off his horse. At that the terrified cattle, already panicked from the sound of the first shots, frantically broke up canyon on a dead run, nearly one hundred steers racing as one. The other mounted rustler, seeing his partner dead and the cattle stampeding straight at him, instantly forgot about anything except escape, and spurred his horse frantically for the arroyo's back trail. One of the men at the campfire dashed for his stomach-shot partner's loose horse, grabbed its reins and leapt into the saddle, then recklessly spurred the mount into the midst of the madly charging cattle in a frenzied attempt to avoid capture or death. Somehow the horse miraculously kept its feet as it was swept along in the stampede.

The rest of the rustlers had dived for cover and were now firing desperately at the lawmen and ranchers. One's bullet clipped a piece of hair from Soot's forelock, then Smoky's return shot took him in the head, the Ranger's slug punching through the man's left eyebrow and burying itself deep in his brain. Another died when Patrick slammed a bullet into his chest. When yet another rustler went down, screeching in agony and terror as Jim's deadly shooting put two bullets through his belly, the two surviving cow thieves quickly threw down their guns and lifted their hands, pleading for mercy.

"Don't … don't shoot any more, please," one of them stammered, as Jim and Smoky aimed their rifles at the captives' chests.

"Just stand hitched," Jim ordered, "One false move and you'll get what your pardners got." Suddenly, out of the corner of his eye he glimpsed Brad Turley and Tom Treloar spurring their horses around the edge of the now milling herd, which had been prevented from running for miles by the canyon's box walls.

"Tom! Brad! Get back here!" Jim shouted.

"We're goin' after those two hombres who got away!" Turley shouted back.

"Forget it!" Jim called after him. "They've got too much of a head start!"

Turley and Treloar ignored the Ranger, spurring their horses harder as they began to climb the narrow trail leading out of the draw. A rifle shot rang out and Treloar jerked in his saddle. A second shot sounded and Turley toppled from his horse. Instantly Treloar leapt off his horse, stumbling as he headed over to the downed cowboy and began dragging him off the trail. Treloar had taken four or five steps when the rifle cracked again and he was slammed to the ground by a bullet plowing into his back. As he fell, the sound of rapidly fading hoofbeats drifted across the draw.

"Sounds like that rifleman took off. I'll go help those boys," Adams volunteered, keeping his rifle at the ready as he swung into his saddle.

"Be careful, Wes," Smoky hollered after him. "I imagine that gunman's taken off by now, but there's still a chance one of those hombres is holed up in those rocks ready to drill anyone who tries to climb that trail."

"I'm ready for him if he tries anything," Adams shouted back as he pushed his sorrel into a trot.

While Smoky kept his rifle leveled at the prisoners, Jim shoved his rifle back in its boot, lifting his Colt from its holster as he dismounted.

"What're you plannin' on doing with us, Ranger?" one of the rustlers stammered as Jim approached them, his pistol pointed straight at their stomachs.

"If it were up to my friends here, you'd be strung up right quick. Bet a hat on it," Jim answered as he nodded at the Normans, who still sat their horses, Ronny clutching his bullet-punctured left arm, while blood dripped from a bullet graze across Patrick's forehead. "But my pard and I are Texas Rangers, so we'll haul you over to Tascola and put you in the jail there until you can stand trial for rustlin' and murder."

Without warning, the man closest to Jim charged him, screaming "I'm not gonna hang," as he grabbed Jim's gun wrist. At the same time, he drove a vicious punch into Jim's gut, driving air from the Ranger's lungs and doubling him up. When Jim staggered against him, the rustler struggled to wrest the heavy Peacemaker from Jim's grasp. As the barrel of the gun was forced downward, Jim managed to thumb back its hammer and pull the trigger. The rustler yelped in surprise and pain, a shocked look of disbelief coming to his face as a .45 slug ripped into his belly and tore through his guts. He stood for a moment, then collapsed in a heap. Seeing his partner fall, the remaining cow thief whirled and took off at a dead run.

"Hold it right there, Mister!" Smoky shouted his order, "Or I'll drop you in your tracks." When the fleeing rustler's only response was a shouted curse and an increase in his speed, Smoky took careful aim and put a bullet into the middle of his back. The rustler stumbled from the impact, staggered a few more steps, then pitched to his face. Smoky calmly shoved his Winchester back into its boot as he glanced over at his partner and softly asked, "Are you all right, Jim?"

"I'm fine," Jim answered, rolling the rustler he'd just shot onto his back. The gutshot renegade gasped as he struggled for a few choked breaths, then violently shuddered, his body twitching for another moment before going completely slack.

"I reckon he was right," Ronny dryly observed as he looked down at the dead man, his hands still clamped to the bullet hole in his middle, "He's not gonna hang."

"I guess that finishes this bunch, except for those two who got into the hills," Patrick Norman stated with satisfaction as he climbed from his mustang and stood at Jim's side to gaze at the rustler's body.

"I reckon it does," Jim bitterly agreed. "If this hombre hadn't gone for my gun he'd still be alive. So would his pardner."

"And they'd be facin' a hang rope in a few weeks anyway," Smoky aggrievedly pointed out. "Jim, I'm goin' to check these hombres to make sure they're all done for. Don't forget those two we just finished were headed for the gallows anyway." As McCue turned away he muttered under his breath so his partner couldn't hear the oaths he directed Jim's way. Smoky quite often got tired of his partner's concern for bringing in alive the outlaws they faced. As far as he was concerned, the ranchers were right. These renegades had stolen cattle and killed several men in doing so. They'd gotten the lead justice they richly deserved.

"I know, but I still don't like it," Jim shrugged.

Jim glanced over at Ronny, who had dismounted and was leaning against his roan, still holding his arm. Blood was seeping between his fingers.

"You'd better let me patch up that arm," Jim told the young rancher.

"It looks like Wes is on his way back with Tom and Brad," Ronny replied as he looked up canyon. "And it seems like Brad's still alive. I'll be okay until you check them."

Adams had gotten both men onto his horse and was now slowly returning, working his way through the cattle which were already settling back to their grazing. Turley was sitting slumped in the saddle, while Treloar was draped belly-down in front of him, over the horse's withers.

"As long as you're sure about that," Jim hesitantly told the young rancher as he watched the approaching trio. Smoky had already checked the bodies of the rustlers and now hurried to help the wounded men.

Once they reached their waiting companions, Adams swiftly dismounted to help Smoky and lift Turley and Treloar from his horse. Blood was dripping steadily from Turley's jaw, while crimson splotched both the front and back of Treloar's faded gray shirt.

"They need some help quick," Adams stated as he and Smoky laid Treloar on the ground, then helped Turley lie down, leaning him against a boulder. "Tom got drilled through the back. Brad took a bullet in his jaw."

"I'll get the medical kits, Jim," Smoky said as Jim hunkered alongside the badly wounded cowpunchers, the rest of the men gathering around.

"How bad is it?" Patrick anxiously asked as Jim quickly examined the men.

"Treloar's in bad shape, but he should pull through if I can get this bleedin' stopped," Jim explained. "That bullet scrape on his neck is just a scratch. The slug which took him in the back went clean through him, and it struck him up high enough so it missed the lungs, looks like."

"What about Brad?"

"Not as bad as it could have been," Jim answered as he examined the wound. "The bullet clipped his chin and glanced off the jawbone, then exited just below his ear. He's lost some blood, and the bone's busted. He'll probably end up with a nasty scar, but he should be all right once he gets to a doc and gets that bone properly set. For now I'll clean up the wound as best I can and immobilize his jawbone so he can't do any further damage."

"Is he gonna be able to talk?" Adams questioned.

"Not for quite some time, I'm afraid," Jim somberly replied. "He'll also be living on soup and coffee for a while, since he won't be able to chew."

"Then maybe the rest of us'll finally be able to get a word in edgewise around the bunkhouse," Adams grinned, relieved that his riding partner was not mortally hit. "Brad, it sure is gonna be peaceful without all your yammerin'," he teased. Turley could only glare at his partner through pain-glazed eyes.

"Here you are, Jim." Smoky handed his partner his canteen, a bottle of whiskey, and a small canvas sack which contained some rudimentary medical supplies.

Jim ripped off Treloar's shirt, exposing the bullet hole in the cowboy's back and the large, ragged exit wound high in his chest. Jim poured water from his canteen over both wounds, sprinkled tobacco into them, and doused them with whiskey. Treloar moaned in pain as the raw liquor hit his torn flesh. Taking two pieces of cloth from the medical kit, Jim stuffed them into the bullet holes. Treloar winced, then his eyes flickered open.

"Take it easy, Tom," Jim ordered.

"What ... what happened?" Treloar weakly murmured.

"You took a bullet in your back," Jim explained. "It went clean through you, but it looks like it missed anything vital, so you should be all right unless blood poisoning sets in. I've cleaned the holes out real good, covered 'em with tobacco and red-eye, then plugged 'em, so I don't think you'll get an infection, at least not right off. But you'll need to get to a doc as soon as you can and get proper treatment."

Treloar chuckled softly despite his intense pain.

"What's so funny, Tom?" Ronny questioned.

"I just thought this is a heckuva way to start a new job, by takin' a slug in my back," Treloar answered, then grunted and passed out.

"He dead, Jim?" Adams asked.

"Nope. Just lost consciousness again. It's better for him that way," Jim replied as he poured more whiskey over the holes in Treloar's chest and back.

"I need someone's shirt," he ordered.

"Take mine." Wes Adams shrugged out of his shirt and handed it to the Ranger. Jim tore it into strips and wrapped them tightly around Treloar's chest and back.

"That should work," Jim grunted as he tied the last strip in place. "Let me see what I can do for Brad."

Efficiently, Jim washed out the bullet holes in Turley's jaw, doused them with the whiskey, and coated them with salve. He then cut the left sleeve off Turley's shirt, tore it into strips, and tied it around the wounded man's head, holding the broken jawbone in place.

"That's the best I can do for now," Jim stated as he knotted the makeshift bandage in place. "Once you these men get back home they'll need to see a doc as soon as possible."

"We'll make sure of that," Patrick promised, then continued to his rider, "Wes, you'd better start ridin' herd on those cows before they get any ideas about runnin' again."

"Hold it just a minute," Jim ordered as he glanced at Adams. "Wes, it looks like you got hit too." The waddy had tied his bloodstained bandanna high on his neck. He also held a blood-stained kerchief pressed to his left ribs.

"These are just scratches," Adams protested. "The bleedin's already stopped. I'm fine."

"Then don't waste any more time," Patrick stated, "Get out with that herd before something spooks 'em. It's gonna be awful hard to hold 'em with one man, but stay with 'em until we can help."

"I'll get right on it," Adams promised. "But what about those two hombres who got away? Aren't we goin' after them?"

"Those men have too big a jump on us," Smoky patiently explained. "Not only that, but from the looks of that trail if we went after them they could just sit up there in the rocks and pick us off one by one. I'm afraid we don't have a snowball's chance in the Mojave of catchin' up with them. But we didn't do all that badly. We took care of most of this bunch, and you've got your cows back."

"I reckon you're right at that," Adams conceded as he swung back into his saddle.

"Hold it one minute, Wes," Patrick ordered.

"Yeah, Pat?" Adams replied.

"It looks like the foreman's job is open again. How would you like to have it?" Patrick asked.

"Not a chance," Adams bluntly responded. "Seems like anyone who takes that job gets his hide punctured by a chunk of lead *muy pronto*. I'll just keep punchin' Rocking N cows."

"I can't say that I blame you," Patrick admitted.

Adams turned his horse and headed back to the milling herd.

"Now you'd better let me patch up that arm," Jim ordered Ronny as Adams rode off.

"It is hurtin' a mite," Ronny allowed.

"I'd guess it is," Jim wryly chuckled. "Roll up your sleeve and let me have a look at it."

"Sure." Ronny rolled his shirtsleeve to the shoulder, revealing two ugly holes in his upper left arm.

"You're lucky," Jim noted. "The bullet went clean through your arm without hitting the bone. I'll just wash out those holes, plug and dress 'em, then bandage you up. You'll be good as new in a few weeks."

Grimacing, Ronny bit his lip against the pain as Jim poured raw whiskey into the bullet holes. "That sure smarts," he muttered as the stinging liquid burned into his torn flesh.

"I know it does, but I've gotta get that wound cleaned out as much as possible so you don't get blood poisoning," Jim answered. "I'll be done in a couple of minutes." He quickly covered the wounds with salve, padded them thickly with gauze, then wrapped a bandage tightly around the young rancher's arm. "There, that's done," he announced with satisfaction. "Just roll down your sleeve, then let me have your bandanna so I can put that arm in a sling. Feel any better?"

"Much," Ronny gratefully replied, as Patrick handing him a bottle of whiskey he'd retrieved from his own saddlebags. "And this'll make it feel even better," he added as he took a long swig of the liquor, then passed the bottle back to his brother, who took a long swallow for himself.

Once Jim had finished tying Ronny's arm in a sling, he turned his attention to Patrick, cleaning and taping a bandage over the shallow bullet gash on his forehead.

"Lieutenant, we appreciate everything you've done for us," Patrick told Jim as he worked on the rancher.

"*Por nada*," Jim answered, "That's what we Rangers are paid for."

"I can't help wonderin' where those renegades would have taken our cows and how they'd get rid of them," Patrick speculated. "We figured our brand was pretty hard to alter."

"They probably were headed for the Territories," Jim answered, "Or maybe they had a buyer who wasn't too fussy about where those cows came from or who owned 'em already lined up. As far as that Rocking N, it wouldn't be too difficult to change it by usin' a running iron to add two lines to turn the N into a box, making it the Rocking Slash Box, or else those lines and another slash, making your Rocking N the Rocking Box X. Any hombre handy with an iron could do it."

"There's pretty much not a brand in Texas that can't be changed by a dishonest cowpuncher who's good with a hot iron," Smoky added.

"You're right about that," Patrick ruefully agreed. "Anyway, thanks again for your help. Will you be heading back to our spread with us? You're more than welcome, anytime."

Jim glanced up at the sun, now well more than halfway past its noon zenith.

"We've got a couple more hours of daylight left, and Smoke and I've still got a lot of miles ahead of us. We'll help you bury these rustlers, then head on out."

"*Bueno,*" Patrick answered. "I reckon we'll spend the night here and rest up, being as this is an ideal spot to keep the herd bunched. They're still a mite spooky from the gunfire. And," he admitted, "we could use some rest ourselves. We'll start out fresh first thing in the morning."

"That's probably best," Jim agreed as he finished taping the bandage in place. "There, I'm finished. Let's get those hombres in the ground."

CHAPTER 8

Until they reached Swanson's Trading Post, Jim and Smoky had been undecided as to where in north Texas they would actually head. While they had settled on either Fort Richardson, outside of Jacksboro, or Fort Griffin as their destination, they still hadn't chosen which Army post to visit. However with Brad Turley's description of the latest stage robbery, which had occurred nearer to Fort Griffin, plus with several of the other crimes having taken place closer to that outpost, the Rangers had finally decided to head for Fort Griffin and its accompanying boomtown. It was several hours after sundown three days later when they rode their weary horses into the town.

"This looks like a lovely little metropolis, Jim," Smoky scornfully observed as they rode along Fort Griffin's single dusty main street. The town appeared to deserve its reputation as one of the toughest in Texas. Most of its occupants were a volatile mixture of outlaws, buffalo hunters, cowboys driving cattle herds north to the Kansas railheads, and cavalry soldiers on leave from the fort. Even an occasional half-breed Comanche or Kiowa could be seen. The buildings were mostly hastily thrown together structures of rough sawn boards, some still merely tents or canvas stretched over wooden frames. Saloons, gambling establishments and brothels seemed to occupy just about every storefront. Before the town's brief history would be played out, more than 200,000 buffalo hides would be shipped from its precincts, and over a twelve year period gunfights would account for thirty-four public killings.[1] However, once the Army abandoned its post the town would quickly decline, and in a few years only a few scattered homesteads along the Brazos River would remain.[2]

"I'll bet my hat no one invites us to high tea, Smo …". Jim's rejoinder was cut short as two long-haired and bearded, rough-visaged men in greasy buckskins tumbled from the door of a saloon and into the street, sprawling practically under Sam and Soot's hooves. Jim had to jerk Sam to such a quick halt that the paint reared, squealing his indignation. As he dropped back down, Sam's teeth snapped as he lunged at the brawling pair, who just managed to roll out of reach of the infuriated horse's bite.

The combatants, buffalo hunters both, struggled mightily in the muddy street, grappling, yelling, and cursing, until one screeched in agony as his opponent drove a knee into his groin. Somehow, despite his pain he managed to come to his knees and pull out a skinning knife from his belt. Believing his adversary paralyzed from the treacherous blow, the other closed in, lunging right into the knife's razor sharp blade. He gasped in shock as the knife was driven deep into his stomach, then reeled backwards as it was jerked out. He clamped a hand to his stomach, blood seeping between his fingers.

Before the Rangers could even react, the gutted hunter pulled out an old cap and ball Colt pistol and shot the other man point-blank in the chest, the impact of the lead at such close range driving his antagonist onto his back in the muck, twitching to stillness. His life rapidly ebbing, the knifed man let his gun fall from his hand, took two wobbly steps, and collapsed with a final long sigh.

Passersby, having learned interference in a fight such as this one between two individuals they didn't know could well lead to their own deaths, hurried past to tend to their business, barely giving the two bodies a second glance.

---

1.   Texas State Historical Records, 2005 Texas State Travel Guide.
2.   Ibid.

"There's nothing we can do here. Let's go, Smoke," Jim ordered, reluctant to reveal their identities as Rangers before meeting with the Army post's commander. As they walked their still snorting horses past the dead men, Jim merely shrugged as he concluded, "I guess sooner or later someone'll pick up those hombres. Let's find a stable for the horses and someplace for ourselves to hole up. We'll visit the fort first thing in the morning."

🍁   🍁   🍁

After finding a livery stable and caring for their horses, the Rangers managed to find a cramped, dirty room in a hastily thrown together building that passed for one of the best hotels in Fort Griffin. The Griffin Manor had been put together in less than a week, built of raw lumber that had dried, warped, and shrunk in the hot sun, leaving many gaps between the thin boards, some almost wide enough to insert a fist. The flimsy partitions between rooms allowed practically no privacy whatsoever. After cleaning up as best they could, Jim and Smoky wolfed down a quick supper, then relaxed over several drinks in the Sharps House Saloon. Slipping into chairs at a corner table, they sat with their backs to the wall and with a clear view of the front door, saying little. In the opposite corner a banjo player perched on a chair placed up on a table, and the jangly twang of his picking cut through the noise of the rip-roaring crowd. From where he sat, Jim could see through the haze of tobacco smoke four games of poker or blackjack going on at nearby tables. As usual, Smoky was eyeing several women mingling with the herd. Surprisingly, no one challenged Jim over his usual choice of libation, sarsaparilla.

"I don't know about you, Smoke, but I'm plumb worn out," Jim finally announced with a yawn and a stretch. "I reckon I'll hit the blankets."

"Same here, pard," Smoky agreed. "I'll have to visit with one of these young ladies tomorrow, after I get some rest."

The exited the saloon and started for their hotel. Halfway across the jostling flood of soldiers, cowboys, and buffalo hunters in the street Smoky stopped short.

"I forgot I'm just about out of tobacco and papers," he announced. "The general store's still open. It won't take me but a minute to fetch some."

"You go ahead," Jim answered, "I'll wait for you by the hotel." Jim continued across the rutted street, stepped up onto the hotel's listing porch, and leaned against the rough wall. He could see Smoky pushing his way through the crowd as he neared the general store.

As the smoke-eyed Ranger strode past a darkened alley a hand shot out and dragged him into the black maw of the narrow passageway. A stray beam of light glinted dully on the barrel of a revolver arcing down at McCue's skull. The gun connected with a sodden thump, caving in the crown of his Stetson. With a soft groan, Smoky slumped to the ground.

Jim's Colt leapt into his hand as he saw his partner pulled out of sight. Glimpsing that downward-arcing gun, he sprang into the street and ran dodging and darting toward the alley. As Smoky's assailant bent over his prostrate form, Jim emerged from the crowd and fired blindly, emptying his revolver at the shadowy figure bending over his friend. The would-be robber and killer was flung violently back as two of Jim's slugs took him in the side, one striking low and tearing into his guts, the other hitting the outlaw high in his side, splintering a rib before passing through a lung to lodge in his heart. The man's limp frame was slammed against the wall, then he dropped without uttering even a final moan of pain.

Jim hurried into the alley and knelt at his downed partner's side, asking as he reloaded his gun, "Smoke, are you all right pard?"

"Guess ... I guess so, Jim," Smoky managed to grunt, struggling to sit up as he pressed one hand to his head. Blood ran freely from an ugly gash ripped open along his scalp.

From out in the street a voice called sharply, "What's going on here?" Jim quickly came to his feet as several soldiers crowded into the alleyway, holding rifles leveled at him.

Jim nodded at the body lying against the store's wall, blood pooling beneath it as he calmly replied, "That hombre over there tried to rob my pardner. He hit him over the head pretty hard. I'm surprised he didn't cave in his skull."

"Perhaps what you say is true, but until all this is straightened out, you're coming with us, Mister. Consider yourself under arrest." The speaker was a young lieutenant whose attempt at a tone of command fell considerably short of his desired effect.

Jim's blue eyes narrowed and grew hard as he growled a reply, his voice low and deadly.

"I'll come with you once my pard's been seen by a doc … but I'm not coming under arrest!"

"You will do as I say, or my men will shoot you where you stand." The officer's voice trembled as it rose in pitch.

"Don't even think about it!" Jim shot back, gazing levelly at the young shavetail, who had made the rookie mistake of standing clearly silhouetted in the mouth of the alley, making himself a clear backlit target. "I've got my Colt aimed just above your shiny belt buckle, Mister, and I can't miss, so if you or any of your men make one false move we'll both die here tonight." Anger in the Ranger's voice added a cold snap to his words.

The lieutenant stood frozen as he realized his tactical and quite possibly fatal error. He realized from the tone of Jim's voice the Ranger meant exactly what he said. One squeeze on the trigger of the gun held in Jim's hand would send a chunk of lead ripping into his guts. The lieutenant's voice quavered slightly as he attempted to regain control, blustering, "You'll come along peaceably to the fort?"

"That was our plan all along," Jim calmly replied. "My pardner and I were headed to see whoever's in charge of the post anyway, the first thing in the morning."

"Well then, you can just plan on doing that tonight." The lieutenant hesitated before adding, "The post surgeon will tend to your partner. Hawley, Morgan, help this man get his friend to the post hospital. Grimaldi, Sorenson, pick up that body. We'll cart it back to the fort for an inquiry."

CHAPTER 9

"It looks like you took quite a knock on the head there, cowboy," Doctor David Gibson, post surgeon at Fort Griffin remarked as he cleaned the gash in Smoky McCue's scalp. "I can't understand why your skull isn't badly fractured or crushed."

"Because it's so thick, doc," Jim Blawcyzk chuckled.

"Jim, I've got enough of a headache as it is," Smoky groaned.

"Well, be that as it may you're a very lucky man," Gibson continued as he wrapped a clean white bandage around the Ranger's head. "However, you'd best take it easy for a couple of days. You've probably received at least a slight concussion, and if you fall off your horse, or take another blow to your head, well...." Doctor Gibson shrugged significantly.

"I'll try and keep him quiet, Doc, but I'm not making any promises," Jim said, "especially with all the saloons and young ladies in this town."

"Unfortunately, you're absolutely correct in your assessment of Fort Griffin," the physician concurred. "I've never seen another such hellhole in all of my assignments with the United States Army. Well liquor, if your friend doesn't partake to excess, and the company of a young lady never hurt anyone. In fact, I'd say those two things just might help speed your partner's recovery."

"See, I told you Jim." Smoky's grin was a mile wide. "You ought to listen to the doc here."

"Never mind that, McCue," Jim grumbled. "I'm a happily married man, as you well know. As far as red-eye, I just don't care for the taste … nor the way it dulls a man's senses just when he needs them the most."

The door to the treatment room swung open, revealing the young lieutenant who had brought the Rangers to the Army post.

"Doctor, is that man patched up?" he gruffly asked.

"As best as I can do for now. He should be observed for a day or so, in case his concussion is more severe than it appears, but he's not going to take my advice about that," Gibson explained.

"Fine. Then I'll take these two along right now," the lieutenant answered.

McCue got up from the table and placed his Stetson awkwardly over his bandaged head. "Let's go," he muttered.

The lieutenant led Jim and Smoky across the fort's parade ground and motioned them up the stairs of a small residence and office as he knocked on the frame of the half-open door.

"Come in, Lieutenant Stovall," a harsh voice replied to the young officer's rap on the door. Eyeing the two Rangers coldly, the owner of that voice, a full colonel, continued, "I assume these are the two men you told me about."

"Yes, sir!" Lieutenant Stovall saluted. "They insisted on meeting with you personally."

"They have no right to insist on anything," the colonel grated. "I only agreed to meet with them out of curiosity, before I have them slapped in irons. From what you have told me, they were involved in at least one murder … and no doubt more we don't know about."

As McCue stood, swaying slightly, the normally placid Blawcyzk's tightly leashed anger finally boiled over.

"Mister," he snarled, "I don't even know your name yet, but I can see you've got a lot to learn, colonel or not."

"How dare you speak to me that way!" the colonel thundered. "I am Colonel Lyndall Thomas, commanding officer in charge of Fort Griffin. You men were caught in the act of committing a crime."

Struggling mightily to regain his composure, Jim coolly responded, "No sir, we were not. My pardner was viciously attacked in an attempted robbery, and I was forced to defend him. You may be in charge of this post, Colonel, but you have no jurisdiction in town. In case you've forgotten, Reconstruction's over. We only have to report to the local marshal. And our authority supercedes his, in case you have any doubts."

"There is no marshal in Fort Griffin at the moment," Thomas tried to explain. "You are no doubt aware that in the absence of local law enforcement the Army has the authority to step in. That is why my men were patrolling the town."

"They didn't do much good, did they?" Jim scathingly answered.

"Easy, Jim," Smoky murmured, vainly attempting to calm his infuriated partner. "Remember why we're here."

"I'm getting to that, Smoke, if we can ever get past this sack of hot air." As Smoky swayed again, Jim added, "You'd better take a seat over there."

"You listen to me, Mister!" While Smoky dropped into a side bench, Thomas' heavy chair fell back as the colonel drew himself up like a fighting cock.

"No, *you* listen to *me*, Colonel," Jim snapped. "My pard and I aren't under your command, although we did come here to meet with you on an urgent and confidential matter. So if you will kindly dismiss the lieutenant, we need to speak in private."

"Sir?" Lieutenant Stovall had never seen anyone defy his commanding officer before. His gaze twitched back and forth between these two difficult men and his commanding officer, who stood stiffly, quivering with anger.

"Give me ten minutes with these men," Thomas ordered. "Then I shall have them shot … or hung!"

Jim flatly contradicted him. "I doubt very much you'll do either."

Once the door had closed behind Lieutenant Stovall, Jim's silver star on silver circle Texas Ranger badge appeared in the palm of his hand.

"What is this? Some kind of trick?" Thomas demanded.

"No tricks, Colonel," Jim explained. "I'm Texas Ranger Jim Blawcyzk, and my pardner there is Smoky McCue. That dead jigger your soldiers brought in jumped Smoky from an alleyway. He won't ever be able to try that on someone else."

Thomas drew back and considered Jim's words a moment before replying, "I take it the Rangers have sent the two of you up here to establish some semblance of law and order in Fort Griffin."

"I wish it were quite that simple." Blawcyzk shook his head. "Unfortunately, we're here on a far more pressing matter. You've no doubt heard of a rash of stagecoach robberies in this vicinity ... in fact, over most of north central Texas."

"Indeed I have," Thomas agreed. "My troops have orders to search for the culprits if at all possible. However, as you know keeping the Comanches in check and on their reservation is our first priority." Thomas' brown eyes still smoldered with barely veiled hostility. Blawcyzk didn't much care. Although Captain Trumbull had requested that Jim and Smoky cooperate with the Army insofar as that was possible, the longstanding Reconstruction era animosity between United States soldiers and local and state officials still bubbled just below the surface. It didn't help matters that the usually easy-going Blawcyzk and the arrogant Thomas had taken an instant dislike to each other.

"And you're doing a fine job at both," Jim mockingly answered. "But we were ordered to here or Fort Richardson because Ranger Headquarters received a disturbing report about one of the most recent holdups. One witness survived just long enough to describe the bandits. He claimed they were United States Army soldiers."

"Impossible!" Thomas angrily flared. "Those highwaymen were obviously impostors or deserters."

"You're quite probably correct." Cooling down somewhat, Jim attempted to smooth the colonel's ruffled feathers. "But we have to consider every angle if we're going to find those renegades. How many of your troops are out on patrol right now ... not counting the men in town, of course."

"Two groups," Thomas explained, "One under Captain John Bosco, the other under Major Thaddeus Stevens."

"Not old 'Iron Jaw' Stevens?" Smoky jerked up in his seat. "He's a fine officer, from what I hear tell. My cousin from Kansas served under him in the War."

"The same," Thomas answered, "And I can assure you no man under my command would be involved in these despicable acts. You can be certain of that, Ranger Blawcyzk."

"I'll take your word on that for now," Jim grudgingly conceded, "Until I come up with evidence to the contrary." As he finished, a soft knock came at the door, followed by Lieutenant Stovall's cautious entrance.

"Sir ...?" Stovall looked questioningly at Colonel Thomas.

"These men are free to go, for the moment," Thomas answered. To the Rangers he added, "But gentlemen, I strongly suggest you leave Fort Griffin at your first opportunity."

"We'll leave when our work is finished," Jim told him. "C'mon, Smoke, let's get out of here."

As they walked through the post's gates Smoky softly chuckled, "Nice job of cooperatin' with the Army there, pardner."

"Hey, we didn't stretch a rope, did we?" Jim laughed. "Besides, that stiff-necked windbag of a colonel wouldn't have cooperated with us no matter what. C'mon, you'd best get some shut-eye and try to get rid of that headache."

CHAPTER 10

As anxious as they were to get back on the trail of the outlaws, Jim and Smoky had little choice but to remain in Fort Griffin for a few days while Smoky recovered from the blow to his head.

Two days after their meeting with Colonel Thomas, they ate supper in the Trail Dust Saloon after taking Sam and Soot out for an afternoon ride to exercise the horses, and also to see if Smoky could tolerate jouncing in the saddle. With their mounts still at the hitchrail outside, the Rangers now sat over a few drinks. Jim nursed his usual sarsaparilla, while Smoky put away a few shots of whiskey. Slightly the worse for wear, he beckoned to a bosomy black-haired saloon girl who'd been eyeing him boldly all evening.

"What's your name, darlin'?" he asked as soon as she reached his side.

"It's Cindy Lou." She stood smiling with her hands on her curving hips, which Smoky had not failed to notice.

"Well, Miss Cindy Lou. I'm Smoky. My pard here's Jim. Care to join us for a drink?"

"I'd love to," she answered in a soft drawl, pulling up a chair next to McCue. "Is there anything else you'd like?" she added. "I could show you something real special."

"As soon as we've had our drink," Smoky smiled in anticipation as he poured a full tumbler of rye for her.

Cindy Lou glanced at Jim as he took another swallow of sarsaparilla.

"What about your silent partner over there?" she queried, "Does he want a gal too?"

"Not Jim. He's got a wife, and he won't have a thing to do with any other woman, no matter how long he's been on the trail." Smoky explained.

"You've got to be joking!" Cindy Lou eyed Jim with a mixture of disbelief and astonishment.

"Nope," Smoky rejoined. "He won't drink, smoke, or cuss either."

"My word." The saloon girl fanned herself. "This is the first time I've ever seen a saint in this place. Next you'll be telling me he goes to church every Sunday."

"He does whenever possible," Smoky said, then added dryly, "But Jim's not exactly a saint. He knows how to use his fists and that gun he's wearin'."

"McCue, if you're headin' upstairs with the young lady, get goin'," Jim half-growled. He didn't need to find himself in the middle of a senseless gunfight started by his partner's whiskey-loosened tongue. "I'll wait for you down here."

"We're goin', Jim … we're goin'." Smoky tossed back the contents of his glass, took Cindy Lou's arm, and allowed her to lead him up the stairs. Jim watched as they disappeared behind the third door along the gallery.

Cindy Lou turned to Smoky as soon as the door had closed behind them, asking if he wanted another drink.

"I sure don't right at this moment, but maybe later," Smoky replied. "Now, Miss Cindy Lou, what's that something special you promised to show me?" He had already shed his Stetson and gunbelts, and sat on the edge of the bed tugging off his boots.

"Just be a little patient, cowboy," Cindy Lou replied as she untied the kerchief from around his neck and draped it around her own, then unbuttoned his shirt and ran her fingers tantalizingly down his chest.

"I've been waitin' long enough already," Smoky retorted as he shrugged out of the shirt. "So what's that unique treat you swore I'd see?"

"I can...." Cindy Lou leaned close to whisper in Smoky's ear.

"You're kidding!" Smoky exclaimed.

"I'm certainly not," Cindy Lou retorted. "And I'm about to prove that to you, right now!" Smoky's blood raced with anticipation as she wrapped her surprisingly gentle arms around him and pressed her lips to his.

❦   ❦   ❦

"You look mighty pleased, Smoke," Jim observed a short while later, as Smoky descended the stairs with Cindy Lou on his arm and returned to where his partner waited. The saloon girl fixed Smoky with a backward lingering glance as she returned to her station by the bar. McCue eased back into his chair, opposite his partner.

"The doc was right, Jim. She cured what ailed me. That gal's really somethin'," Smoky readily admitted. He grinned with pleasure as he rolled another cigarette, stuck it between his lips, and lit it.

"Well that's good. Maybe you'll finally be better company," Jim joked. "C'mon, let's get outta here. Maybe we can finally get after those renegade soldiers or whatever they are first thing tomorrow. And it's high time we got the horses back to the stable."

As the two lawmen emerged from the Trail Dust several riders burst around the corner, spurring their horses down the crowded main street at a full gallop. Sudden gunfire caused a stampede as the marauders cut loose at anyone in sight. A pair of dusty cowpokes, joking and laughing as they stepped onto the saloon's porch, were both shot dead, falling at the Rangers' feet.

Jim and Smoky instinctively ripped out their Colts and began blazing away at the rampaging riders. Several men fell from their saddles as Ranger slugs sought out their vitals. Jim dropped at least three before he broke for the opposite side of the street to catch the gunmen in a crossfire. Blood soaked into the dirt of the road as men and horses whirled in confusion, some of the riders diving from their saddles to seek cover.

"Cover me, Smoke!" Jim shouted as he zigzagged through the melee, gun blasting, finally lunging behind the shelter of a horse trough to reload.

Smoky emptied both of his pistols into the bunched-up horsemen, then leapt to the hitch rail where Soot stood pawing and rolling his eyes and pulled his Winchester from its saddle boot. At that instant Jim put his last bullet through the middle of a paunchy, florid faced raider. The gunman screamed, then cursed Jim viciously as he clamped both hands to his belly and crumpled to the boardwalk.

Smoky staggered as a bullet clipped his shoulder, and he went to one knee alongside Soot. Over the noise of gunfire, the screaming of terrified horses and cursing men, he heard a frustrated "Dadblast it!" as Jim's six-gun hammer clicked on an empty chamber.

Two surviving raiders had wheeled their mounts and were galloping back down the street in a desperate bid for escape. Blawcyzk dove to his belly as slugs struck all around him, smashing out a window behind him and blasting holes through the trough. Smoky struggled upright to shout, "Jim, here!" as he tossed his partner his rifle.

Jim snatched the Winchester in mid-flight, brought it smoothly to his shoulder, and fired. His bullet struck one of the fleeing renegades low in his back, tearing through his body to emerge just above the belt buckle. As the outlaw arched backward from the impact, the tumbling slug clipped the top of his horse's head and the stunned animal went down, trumpeting in terror. His rider was trapped in the saddle, crushed between the road and a thousand pounds of horseflesh as his mount fell. The horse regained its feet and trotted away blowing and trembling, leaving the raider flattened in the dirt.

Before the first renegade had even hit the ground, Jim worked the Winchester's lever, switched aim, and pulled the trigger. Smoke and flame erupted from the gun's muzzle, and the bullet struck the last flee-ing raider squarely between his shoulderblades. With a scream of pain the man sagged across his horse's neck, grasping frantically at its mane. His pitching chestnut bucked to the right, sending his rider slewing out of the saddle. Boot caught in the stirrup, the outlaw's body was dragged around the corner and out of sight by the panicked, runaway mustang.

Smoky whirled around too late at the click of a revolver's hammer behind him. A young outlaw stood there, eyes wide in his dust smeared face as he grinned in triumph, leveling his pistol at the Ranger's broad chest. The sneering gunman was just about to squeeze his trigger when an object dropped from above landed directly on his head, caving in his skull and snapping his neck, killing him instantly as he was slammed flat. The renegade's finger reflexively closed on the trigger, but his shot went wild as he fell. The dead young desperado appeared broken into as many pieces as the heavy flowerpot that had smashed squarely onto his head. Smoky glanced upward, glimpsing only a vague figure disappearing behind gently moving curtains.

"You okay, Smoke?" Jim raced up to his partner as a rare silence descended on Fort Griffin. Smoky was still staring at the body of the man who'd nearly put a bullet in his chest. Jim handed Smoky back his Winchester, removed six cartridges from Smoky's gunbelt, and began calmly reloading his Colt.

"I'm just scratched Jim, thanks to whoever beaned that s.o.b.", Smoky reassured him.

"Smoky, you're all right!" Cindy Lou shouted as she burst through the batwings of the Trail Dust and rushed up to McCue to wrap him in a huge embrace. She gasped, her eyes widening in fear as she spotted his blood drenched shoulder and exclaimed, "No! You're hurt!"

"I'm just grazed. It ain't nothin," Smoky muttered, "Could've been a mite worse. With his rifle still in one hand and his other arm around Cindy Lou, he looked her straight in the eye and questioned, "Did you drop the flowerpot on that jigger's head?"

"That I certainly did," Cindy Lou confessed, shuddering only slightly as she glanced at the body. The mask of blood coating the dead man's face matched the scarlet blaze of the flowers spilling from the shattered adobe pot. Cindy Lou smiled weakly at the Ranger as she requested, "Smoky, can you get my flowers back? I'd like to repot them."

"Sure I can, honey," Smoky softly replied.

"Smoke …" Unable to resist a joke, no matter how bad or macabre, Jim grinned wickedly, suppressing a chuckle.

"What, Jim?"

"I guess you might say that hombre's got a geranium in his cranium, thanks to your lady friend there. And also thanks to your lady friend he's certainly potted."

"Jim, you …" Smoky growled, whatever oath he was about to hurl at his partner cut short by the sound of approaching hoofbeats. They turned to gaze at a column of blue clad riders drawing near.

"What in blue blazes went on here?" Colonel Lyndall Thomas, at the head of the column of troopers, demanded as he dismounted and strode purposefully up to where Blawcyzk, McCue, and Cindy Lou stood. The colonel stopped short as he recognized the Rangers. *"You two!"* he exploded. "I'm sure you must have some explanation for this. I'm waiting to hear it."

"We don't know ourselves just what this was all about, Colonel," Jim calmly replied. "A bunch of hombres just started shootin' up the town for no reason, it seems like, and pluggin' anyone who got in their way. Smoky and I stopped them … well, most of 'em, anyway. A couple of them got away. It's too bad you and your soldiers couldn't have gotten here a little sooner. We could have used some help."

Thomas ordered his troopers to secure the street, then turned back to the Rangers with grudging respect in his eyes.

"Well, you seem to have done all right for yourselves," he reluctantly conceded. "For the moment, I'll accept your version of what happened here. I was going to send a man to summon you to the fort anyway. Now you've saved me the bother. I have a telegram for you, sent by your commanding officer in Austin, in case you rode up this way." He handed Jim the yellow telegraph flimsy. "And might I ask why you neglected to provide me your rank the other night, Lieutenant Blawcyzk?"

"I don't usually announce that, unless I have to," Jim explained, "And I thank you for bringing us that wire."

"You're quite welcome, Lieutenant," Thomas curtly responded. "And if I were you, I'd see to your partner's wound. My men can take care of this situation."

"It's hardly a scratch, Colonel," Smoky shrugged.

"Still, the Colonel's right, Smoke," Jim said, as he perused the telegram. "C'mon, let's put up the horses and get back to our room. I can clean out that bullet scrape. There's no need for the doc."

"Can't I help take care of him?" Cindy Lou plaintively cried.

"Yeah, Jim. Can't she?" Smoky echoed.

"Not tonight, Smoke." Jim shot his partner a warning glance. "In fact Cindy, you'd be safer if you stayed off the street for the rest of the night. I'll make sure Smoky comes to see you tomorrow ... not that I think he'll need much encouragement," he chuckled.

Quickly their horses were put away, rubbed down and fed, Sam getting his usual peppermint, and the Rangers returned to their hotel.

"All right, Jim. What's in that telegram?" Smoky demanded as soon as they were settled in their room.

"Take off your shirt pard, and I'll let you read it while I patch you up," Jim answered, as he dug in his saddlebags for a clean cloth and a tin of salve.

While Jim wet the cloth with tepid water from a chipped clay pitcher, which along with two sagging, battered beds made up the entire furnishings of their room in one of the finest hostelries in Fort Griffin, Smoky eased onto the edge of his bed and tugged off his blood-spattered shirt. The bullet which had clipped him had left only a shallow groove burned across the top of his right shoulder. Wincing silently as Jim cleaned the wound, Smoky scanned the telegram from Captain Trumbull twice before looking up and softly whistling.

"It seems our boys have graduated and are goin' after bigger game," he commented.

"It sure looks that way," Jim agreed as he salved Smoky's shoulder. As he bandaged the bullet slash with a clean strip of cloth, he added, "We've got to track 'em down and stop 'em, right quick."

CHAPTER 11

Late in the evening of the day following Blawcyzk's and McCue's arrival in Fort Griffin, two dusty-clothed men bought tickets on a westbound train at Denton. Besides the three passenger coaches, a single box car, and a caboose, immediately behind the locomotive's tender was an express car which carried thousands of dollars in specie for several Texas banks. Just before departure, the pair approached the express car through the gathering twilight. One was a tall, commanding figure, his colleague shorter and huskily built.

"Hold it right there, both of you!" A pipe smoking messenger just inside the car's half-opened door leveled his sawed-off shotgun at the approaching men. A shadow cast by the single wall lamp in the car disclosed his partner's position further inside, away from the open door and any direct line of fire.

"Easy, gentlemen, please," the taller man spoke soothingly. "We intend no harm. Allow us to show you our credentials." His voice was strong, confident, and reassuring.

"All right, but move slow and careful. One false move and I'll blow the both of you in two," the guard cautiously replied. Pipesmoke wreathed his shaded features as he edged back from the door.

Reaching carefully inside his vest, Major Thaddeus Saunders extracted his Army commission and passed it up to the guard, along with a set of orders he himself had carefully forged.

"Major Saunders? I don't understand, sir," the guard wondered as he gazed at the officer's dirt smeared face with its three day's growth of whiskers. Despite his puzzlement, the messenger's shotgun never wavered as he kept its twin barrels aimed point-blank at the newcomers' stomachs.

"It's quite simple, Mr...."

"Jake. Jake Castle."

"Jake. As I said, it's quite simple. Trooper Hank Brady and I have been assigned as extra guards to make certain your ... 'cargo' reaches its destination safely," Saunders smoothly explained. "And obviously we don't wish to advertise our presence by being in uniform."

"What do you think, Charlie?" Jake doubtfully asked his partner.

"It sounds all right to me, Jake," Charlie Hunt, the other messenger assented. "All this cash has got me jumpy as a hound dog loaded with fleas. I sure won't mind havin' a couple of soldier boys along to help us out."

"If you have any doubts, let me assure you the shipment will be in good hands until it's unloaded," Saunders mildly added.

"I guess it's all right then, Major," Jake acquiesced. "You and Trooper Brady climb aboard."

As the locomotive's whistle blew and the conductor shouted his "All Aboard!" Saunders and Brady scrambled into the express car. Once they were inside, Jake slammed the door shut and bolted it from the inside. When the train huffed into motion, the men settled down for the long westward haul.

At a whistle stop in Decatur, two more out of uniform soldiers in Saunders' command boarded the train, taking seats in the forward passenger coach, which was immediately behind the express car. One, stocky and dressed in a railroader's rough work clothes, found an aisle seat next to the front door, stretched out and pulled his hat low over his eyes, then quickly fell asleep. The other, slender and fair, clad in a drummer's cheap suit and derby hat and limping heavily, settled into a seat a few rows back, gazing silently out the window as the train rumbled southwestward. He became more alert as the train began climbing through the broken hills and breaks of the Brazos River country. Sometime later, when the locomotive started laboring up a long grade he rose from his seat to shuffle slowly and deliberately through the car, passing quietly out the front door and onto the forward platform. A few passengers gazed curiously at him, but on the assumption he was just stepping outside for a breath of air or to have a smoke no one questioned his move. The other soldier never moved, ostensibly not even stirring as the erstwhile drummer left the coach.

Once outside, the slender trooper swiftly stepped across the gap to the express car's platform and withdrew a hooked length of heavy wrought iron from the right leg of his trousers. Hanging precariously by one hand from the platform railing, he threaded the hook through the ring atop the coupler pin and tested the slack. On this long upgrade there was none at all with the weight of three passenger coaches, a box car and a caboose dragging behind. The iron rod vibrated in his hand as the train clacked across sections of rail, smoke and cinders swirling around the cars. For long moments the soldier hung low over the tracks, waiting for the grade to level off. Finally sensing a slight easing of the tension on the pin, he gave a sharp whistle. At that signal, the other trooper left his seat to join his partner on the express car's platform. Seconds later the coupling slackened as the following cars crested the grade. With a decisive upward jerk the slim soldier yanked the pin clear of the drawhead, uncoupling the passenger coaches, boxcar, and caboose from the rest of the train. The cars slowly lost forward momentum as the locomotive, tender, and express car pulled away. Now on a slight downgrade, they rolled to almost a complete halt, then began to pick up speed when they rumbled onto a steeper section of roadbed. Passengers jerked upright in their seats as the cars began to roll unimpeded down the grade.

In the caboose the two brakemen jumped to their feet as they felt the cars slow, then begin to gain momentum.

"What the devil is goin' on, Ben?" one shouted.

"We've come unhooked from the rest of the train, that's what, Josh!" the other exclaimed. "We've gotta try and stop this thing, fast. If we can't before we hit that curve by the trestle at Hennessey's Gulch we're done for!" He and his partner dashed out of the front door of the caboose to head for the handbrake wheels at the end of each car.

While the brakemen scrambled over the car roofs in their desperate attempt to stop the train before it plunged into Hennessey's Gulch, passengers braced themselves for a horrendous crash, many praying, several women screaming or crying in fear. The cars lurched sickeningly as they rocketed around several gradual downhill curves, their speed steadily increasing. Ben, frantically manhandling the brake wheel on the caboose, was nearly flung to his death as the runaway cars tilted precariously on the tracks. Metal screeched as wheels rode up on the rails, then miraculously settled back.

Desperately fighting the stubborn resistance of the handbrakes, Ben finally managed to set the brakes of the caboose, while Josh, who had crawled on hands and knees to the foremost coach, was able to lock that car's brakes in place. Hot lengths of metal shavings were torn from the rails, the wheels and tracks screaming their torment as the runaway finally shuddered to a halt. Josh rolled onto his back, trembling and sweating, then dropped to the ground, while Ben shakily climbed from the roof of the caboose, his knees wobbly as he reached the ground and started for the passenger cars.

Passengers began streaming from the coaches before the two crewmen could step inside. They glanced at the looming maw of Hennessey's Gulch, less than a hundred yards ahead, then at the brakemen and broke into spontaneous applause for the men who had just saved their lives.

"What in blazes?" Jake exclaimed as he felt the express car suddenly lunge forward when the rearmost cars were uncoupled and the engine leapt ahead under its much lighter load. He grabbed the shotgun which he had leaned against the padlocked express box and leapt to his feet. His shout of consternation was cut short as in one smooth motion Major Saunders drew his saber from beneath his shabby duster and rammed it deep into the guard's belly. The razor-sharp steel sliced cleanly through Jake's intestines as Saunders ran him through. Jake grabbed futilely at Saunders, ripping away a strip of the major's sleeve as he sagged over the blade, then crumpled to the floor when the major ripped the saber from his middle. Blood pooled around the guard's still twitching body.

Before Charlie Hunt could react, Trooper Brady yanked out his Bowie and sank the knife deep between Hunt's ribs, thrusting the blade upward through the stomach to pierce the heart. Hunt's mouth opened for a scream that would never come as he collapsed to sprawl unmoving alongside his partner.

"Quick Brady, get that door open!" Saunders ordered as he stooped to retrieve a ring of keys from Jake's vest pocket. Brady nodded as he stepped to the padlocked door, using the heavy blade of his bloody knife to wrench the padlock and its hasp from the door frame. He yanked open the door to admit his two confederates to the car.

"Morton, Ronson, you know what to do," Saunders ordered as the two men entered the car. "Be quick about it. The rest of the men are waiting just ahead."

"Yes sir, Major!" Trooper Stuart Morton replied. Brady had already unlocked the car's front door, and seconds later Morton and Private Pete Ronson were scrambling across the cordwood piled high in the tender. The train's sweating fireman had just turned and grabbed another chunk to toss in the roaring firebox when he spotted the two men, guns in hand, climbing over the split lengths. He drew back his arm to throw the length of wood he held at Ronson's head, but was stopped short as Morton shot him through the stomach. Flung backwards by the close range bullet, the fireman was slammed into the locomotive cab's wall, then pitched from the engine to slide down the trackbed's steep embankment. His body's plunge was finally halted by a thick patch of prickly pear.

When Morton shot the fireman, Ronson drew a bead on the engineer's back and pulled the trigger of his revolver twice. The trainman arched in pain as two slugs ripped low into his back, then half-spun before collapsing to the engine's sooty metal floor.

Both men jumped down from the woodpile, Ronson kicking the engineer's body aside as Morton grabbed the locomotive's throttle and shoved it forward to slacken speed. He then hauled back hard on the brake lever, bringing the train to a shuddering stop. As it ground to a halt, several uniformed men on horseback emerged from a gully, leading extra mounts.

"You did good work, all of you," Saunders shouted as he and Brady shoved open the heavy side door and kicked the messengers' remains to he dirt. "Everything's gone perfectly so far. Now hurry and get this cargo unloaded."

Sergeant Duffy, who'd been leading the mounted men, dropped from his saddle to clamber up into the express car. Saunders handed him the ring of keys he'd taken from Jake Castle's body. It took several tries before Duffy found the key which fit the strongbox's heavy padlock.

"Got it!" Duffy triumphantly hissed as the key slid easily into the lock and it popped open. The sergeant yanked off the lock and flipped open the box's lid, staring greedily at its contents.

"Look at all that *dinero!*" Brady hissed from his place at the door.

"Never mind about that now!" Saunders ordered. "Get busy!"

Working feverishly, the troopers soon had the gold off-loaded and distributed among their saddlebags. Less than half an hour later they rode away from the blood-spattered cars, back up the gully and onto a hardpan plain that would reveal little sign of their passing. They rode hard all night, not stopping until just before dawn, when they paused at a shallow creek to water and rest their horses and wolf down a quick, cold breakfast. Saunders and his disguised cohorts discarded and burned their civilian outfits, scrubbing themselves thoroughly and shaving the scraggly beards from their faces before changing back into their blue Army uniforms. Miles behind them, a gutted express car and a locomotive, smoke still dribbling forlornly from its diamond stack, stood as mute testimony of the death they had wrought.

CHAPTER 12

Fortunately Smoky's wound was not incapacitating, so the two Rangers departed Fort Griffin well before dawn the next morning, in their haste Smoky even neglecting to leave a note of explanation for Cindy Lou. Two days of hard riding later they walked their horses down the main street of Graham, where the ill-fated locomotive and express car had been hauled. Leaving the worn-out Sam and Soot hitched in front of the town marshal's office with a brief apology, peppermints for both, and a promise to care for them as soon as possible, the two partners brushed trail dust from their clothes as they stepped onto a weathered porch and through the office's open door.

"Can I help you gentlemen?" From behind a scuffed pair of boots propped on a battered desk, the office's lone occupant glanced up sleepily at his visitors. Their glinting badges brought him leaping to his feet.

"Rangers! Thank God you're here!" he blurted. "I'm Marshal Brian Wood. I expect you've come about the train robbery."

"That's right, Marshal," Jim confirmed. "I'm Jim Blawcyzk, and this is my pardner, Smoky McCue. Austin wired us about the holdup, and said the train had been brought here. We'll want to see it right away."

"Sure thing, Ranger," Wood readily agreed. "Just let me get my horse and I'll take you down to the railyard. The Texas Northern sent a railroad detective all the way up here from Houston. I reckon we'll find him down at the yard too."

Wood retrieved his grulla gelding from the small corral behind his office and rejoined the Rangers, who had already swung back into their saddles.

"Any idea who might've pulled off the robbery?" Smoky inquired as they trotted toward the tracks.

"Nary a one," Wood ruefully admitted. "There's not much to go on, as far as I can tell."

"Any witnesses?" Jim queried.

"As far as the robbery itself, no," Wood explained. "You see, the passenger coaches and caboose were unhooked from the rest of the train. They rolled down a long grade. Nearly were wrecked at Hennessey's Gulch, but the two brakemen managed to stop those cars just before they would've derailed and gone off the trestle and into the gulch. That's more'n a hundred foot drop, so if those coaches had derailed there most likely wouldn't have been a soul ridin' in them left alive."

"So those hombres wanted to kill everyone on the train," Smoky mused.

"Seems so," Wood agreed. "That way there wouldn't have been anyone alive to talk."

"You said there weren't any witnesses to the robbery itself," Jim took up. "What'd you mean by that, Marshal?"

"Folks in the first passenger car said a couple of hombres got up and stepped out onto the front platform just before the cars were uncoupled," Wood explained as they arrived at the small Graham depot. "But you'd be better off askin' the T-N's detective about that. Here we are. I'd better let the station agent know you're here." The trio of lawmen dismounted, looped their horses' reins over the hitchrail, and pushed through the door into the depot. A red-faced man with huge burnsides rose to greet them.

"Marty, these are Texas Rangers Blaw … Blah … heck, how'd you say your name again, Ranger?" Wood stumbled.

"It's B-l-a-w-c-y-z-k, pronounced 'Bluh-zhick'," Jim grinned, used to people getting tongue-tied with his Polish surname. "Lots easier if you just call me Jim."

"Jim it is," Wood readily agreed. "So it's Rangers Jim and McCue."

"Call me Smoky," McCue added, "And Jim here's a Ranger lieutenant, though he doesn't readily admit to that."

"Okay, Smoky. And I'm Brian. This here's Marty Stockard, the Texas Northern station agent," the marshal introduced. "Marty, that detective still out back?"

"The last I knew," Stockard idly shrugged as he shifted the chaw of tobacco in his cheek. "He was still goin' over that baggage car. You know the way back there, Marshal."

"I reckon I do," Wood retorted. "C'mon Jim, Smoky. I'll take you out back."

The three lawmen stepped out the back door of the station to the tracks.

"That's her." Wood pointed to a locomotive, tender, and express car shunted onto a siding. As they approached he called out, "Wehner!" An exceptionally tall red-haired man, taller still than the lanky, six foot plus Blawcyzk, and even fairer of complexion than the blond Ranger, poked his head out of the express car's side door.

"Mornin', Marshal." Jeff Wehner's somewhat stern face broke into an unexpectedly warm grin. "You're out and about bright and early."

"I brought you a couple of visitors, Jeff. Texas Rangers Jim Blaw … Blawcy … ah, forget it! Rangers Jim and Smoky."

"Ranger Lieutenant Jim Blawcyzk, and my pardner, Corporal Smoky McCue." As Jim finished Wood's introduction, Wehner jumped from the car and took his hand in a friendly but bone-crushing grip, his pale, narrowed eyes studying the Ranger shrewdly. Jim's steady blue eyes met Wehner's scrutiny unflinchingly.

"Good to meet you both," Wehner replied as he turned to shake hands with Smoky. "I assume you were sent here on account of this holdup. I know the railroad wired Ranger Headquarters about it."

"That's correct," Jim affirmed. "We've been investigating the string of stage holdups in these parts, and our captain seems to feel those same renegades might've decided to try for bigger game."

"Your captain give you any particular reason why he feels that way? And call me Jeff."

"As long as you call us Jim and Smoky," Blawcyzk grinned. "I guess it's just a gut feeling on Captain Trumbull's part, mainly because the stage robbers have killed everyone they've stolen from and been mighty vicious about it. From the little he said in his wire, this train robbery sounds like pretty much the same method."

"Well then, your captain's got the same hunch I have," Wehner rejoined. "C'mon, let's go over the cars. Maybe one of you can come up with something I've overlooked."

"I've got to be getting back to the office," Marshal Wood stated. "Jim, Smoky, as soon as you're done with Jeff come back over there. There's a good stable for your horses right across the street, and I'll have coffee boilin'."

"That sounds good, Brian," Smoky readily agreed. "It's been a hard run over here."

"Then I'll see you in a bit," Wood grinned, as he started back for the depot.

As they scrambled into the express car Jim asked the detective, "Wehner, huh? I recall when I first started Rangerin' I met a sheriff by that same name up in Clay County. He kin of yours by any chance, Jeff?"

"That'd be my dad, Joe Wehner," Jeff replied. "He was sheriff up there for quite a few years. He retired a while back, and spends most of his time with my mom, just gardening and taking life easy."

"I'm glad to hear that," Jim answered. "He was a real decent fella, as I recollect."

"Thanks," Jeff said, as he pointed out several dried blood smudges on the walls of the car, several more on pieces of baggage, and two rusty brown smears caked on the floor where the guards had died. "You can see the guards never had a chance. They didn't even fire a shot."

"How'd the robbers get inside this car?" Smoky wondered.

"That's the big puzzle," Wehner admitted. "We know the rest of the train was uncoupled, so a couple of those renegades likely got through the door from the first coach. What I can't figure is why the two men on guard didn't blast them as soon as they came through the door."

"How about the bodies?" Smoky mused. "Any clues there?"

"No." The detective shook his head. "They'd both been shoved out alongside the tracks. Whoever robbed this train was smart enough to cut the telegraph wires before they pulled the job, so it was quite a while before the holdup was even discovered. By the time anyone got out here, the coyotes and buzzards had pretty well torn the bodies apart. We did find the tracks of a bunch of horses, but they petered out about two miles up a gully."

"What about this?" Jim picked up a ragged strip of dark colored cloth, stained with several spots of dried blood. "Looks like it was torn from one of the robber's coats ... I'd guess by one of your guards."

"That's what I figure too," Wehner concurred, "But you can be sure whoever was wearing the garment that came from has long since shed it. That cloth won't be much help."

"Maybe not, but let's not discount anything," Jim replied. "Well, there's not much more in here. Let's look at the engine cab. That just might give us some clues."

Smoky glanced narrowly at his partner but said nothing as he noticed Jim's slight shake of the head. The jumped down from the express car and clambered into the locomotive's cab.

"The fireman got nailed in his stomach. We found what was left of him tangled in a bunch of prickly pear cactus halfway down an embankment," Wehner explained. "The engineer took two slugs in his back. His body was still inside the cab."

"You say they were both shot? At close range?" Jim questioned as he squatted down to study the locomotive's firebox.

"As near as I can tell," Wehner said. "Both slugs went right through the engineer. And here," he indicated a relatively shiny gouge in the firebox's metal, "This mark looks like it was made by the bullet which killed the fireman."

"I'll agree with you so far, Jeff." Jim regarded the three bullet scars on the firebox, one higher and deeper than the others. He pointed to the shiny indentation. "You can see this one made a deeper dent when it hit. That means it almost certainly didn't hit any bone on its way through the fireman's body." Jim straightened up. "These other two marks are from the bullets that got the engineer."

"You've got an idea Jim, don't you?" Smoky dryly asked.

"Yep." Jim gruffly replied. "Jeff, any signs of slugs in the express car, or in the guards' bodies?"

"None in the bodies. I told you they were pretty torn up by scavengers, Jim," Wehner reiterated.

"How about in the car?"

"None that I saw," the Texas Northern detective admitted.

"C'mon, let me show you something," Jim ordered. Quickly, they climbed out of the locomotive and back into the express car.

"Look here." Jim pointed to the side of a heavy, blood-smeared leather trunk.

"By gosh, I'd missed that!" Wehner exclaimed. "So you think …?"

"I think the guards were stabbed to death, and at least one of 'em had a saber run through his belly," Jim explained. "It had to be a saber or a similar weapon to go clean through him and dig into the trunk that way, and it had to be shoved in low for the blade to leave a mark at that level and that angle. I'd guess the guard grabbed the sleeve of whoever killed him while he was bein' stabbed. That's where that piece of cloth came from."

"But that still doesn't tell us how the killers got in the car," Wehner objected.

"I think I can provide the answer to that," Smoky murmured.

"Go ahead, Smoke," Jim urged.

"Jeff, you know we've been lookin' for men who are possibly Army troops in connection with these robberies and killin's, or at least men masquerading as soldiers," Smoky began. "Now, suppose a couple of them had papers saying they were soldiers sent to help guard this shipment."

"Then our men would most likely have let them in the car," Wehner reluctantly admitted.

"And a couple more of those hombres would have been riding in the coaches, waiting for the right time and place to cut loose the rest of the train. Once that was done the ones in this car killed your guards and let their pardners in. As soon as the guards were taken care of then the engine crew was killed, and one of the robbers drove the train to where the rest of the gang was waitin'. They looted the strongbox, loaded the money into their saddlebags, and rode off," Smoky concluded.

"Smoky's got it pretty much summed up," Jim agreed. "The only thing that seems to have gone wrong for 'em is that the rest of the cars didn't derail into Hennessey's Gulch and kill the rest of the passengers as they'd planned. If this really is a bunch of renegade soldiers, they sure couldn't afford to leave any witnesses. They sure wouldn't be happy about those cars not bein' wrecked. Jeff, Marshal Wood said we should ask you about two men passengers saw leave the first coach just before it was uncoupled."

"Unfortunately, there wasn't much the passengers could tell me," Wehner regretfully answered. "All they saw was a couple of men, one dressed like a railroader, the other like a none-too-successful drummer. Nobody paid any mind to 'em until after those cars were unhooked."

"No other description at all?" Jim queried.

"Only that one was stocky and brown haired, the other thin and blonde," Wehner shrugged. "Heck, that describes just about every man in Texas. And the thin one had a limp, but I've already figured out that was probably because he had an uncoupling rod hidden down his pants leg. So looking for a man with a limp won't help any."

"I've gotta admit you're right about that," Jim conceded.

"And if our men are soldiers, you can be sure they weren't in uniform, just in case anyone did survive the wreck," Smoky added.

"You're right," Jim agreed. "I'm sure they wouldn't have had too hard a time convincing the guards they were traveling incognito."

"And soldiers could easily have forged orders. They also carry sabers, which fits in with your theory of how the guard was killed." Wehner put in, with a look of triumph on his face.

"Exactly," Jim replied. "Now all we have to do is figure out when and where they'll hit next."

CHAPTER 13

"I reckon I'll stop by the Western Union office and get a wire off to the T-N's main office in Dallas," Wehner decided as they left the railyard. "I want to find out when the next big shipment of cash is being transported, and on which train."

"That's a good idea, Jeff," Jim agreed. He and Smoky had both taken a quick liking to the gangly railroad detective. "Smoke, we'll send a wire to Captain Trumbull and let him know what we've come up with. Maybe he'll have some more information for us."

Once their telegrams were sent, the Rangers and railroad detective headed for the marshal's office, where they settled into battered chairs, leaning them back against the wall.

"Any luck, Jim?" Wood asked as he poured the Ranger a mug of steaming black coffee and handed it to him.

"Some clues, but nothing definite," Jim replied while Wood passed mugs of the thick brew to Smoky and Wehner. "Jeff's hoping the Texas Northern can provide us some more information."

"And I expect to have that before the telegraph office closes for the night," Wehner broke in.

"I sure hope you do," Jim observed. "Brian, while we're waiting, you said the stable across the way's a good place to put up our horses?"

"It sure is," Wood confirmed. "See old Dave MacTavish over there. He'll take good care of your broncs. Jeff brought his horse up from

Houston and he's stabled over there." The Texas Northern detective nodded his agreement.

"Jim's always more worried about our horses than ourselves," Smoky chuckled. When Jim didn't deny that, knowing there was at least some truth in his partner's statement, Smoky continued, "How about a place we can get some grub for ourselves, and maybe a room for the night?"

Wood rubbed his jaw thoughtfully. "Wetmore's restaurant ain't worth the grease he wastes on the food, and callin' the hotel a real dump is being mighty charitable. Jeff took the last decent room left in town, at the widow Benson's boarding house."

"It sounds like we'll be bedding down behind the livery stable," Jim noted. "That's not a problem. We've done it plenty of times before."

"There's no call for that," Wood objected. "I'll tell you what. I can fry up a mean mess of bacon and flapjacks, or a decent stew for supper. I bunk in the back room. You two can either sleep in the cells or roll out your blankets right on the floor. How about it?"

"That sounds all right by me, Brian," Smoky responded. "That okay with you, Jim?"

"It suits me just fine," Jim indifferently replied. "Let's not plan on getting too comfortable, though. Once Jeff gets that answer from the Texas Northern, I've a hunch we'll have some more hard ridin' ahead of us." He drained the last of his coffee, then placed the mug on the marshal's battered desk. "We'd better get our horses rubbed down and fed. They've been standin' at that rail too long already, and with any luck we'll need them before morning."

"Told you Jim worries more about those horses," Smoky grinned as he pushed himself up from his chair. "Gentlemen, we'll see you in a bit."

"I'm sorry, Sam," Jim apologized to his paint as the tired and hungry horse whickered to him inquiringly, then nuzzled his chest. "You're gonna be taken care of right now." He slipped the gelding a peppermint as he lifted the reins from the rail and headed the horse across the street, Smoky and his steeldust alongside.

"Those are without a doubt two of the finest cayuses I've ever seen enter this barn," Dave MacTavish exclaimed, examining the horses as the

Rangers led their mounts into his stable. The wizened old cowboy's deep blue eyes gleamed his appreciation of the fine mounts. "I'll give 'em the best care possible. Whoa there, fella!" MacTavish yelped as he made the mistake of reaching for Sam's reins. Jim's paint stretched out his neck to take a quick nip at the hostler's belly, just missing as MacTavish instinctively bent in the middle. "Okay, I can see you're a one man horse," he muttered. "Ranger, you can get his feed and rub him down."

"I'm sorry, Dave," Jim apologized. "I wasn't quick enough to warn you that Sam won't let anyone touch him unless I say it's all right." To his horse he sternly continued, "Sam, you behave yourself. And apologize to Mr. MacTavish." As Sam dubiously eyed his rider, liquid brown eyes rolling in their sockets to show the whites, Jim ordered again, "I mean it, Sam. You tell him you're sorry." Sam, after a slight snort of protest, lowered his head and nickered softly. When MacTavish tentatively scratched his ears, Sam sighed with contentment.

"That's better, you." Jim gave the gelding another peppermint.

"You've got a rare one there, Ranger," MacTavish observed. "Full grainin' and rubdown?"

"Rare isn't the word," Jim chuckled. "One of these days I'm gonna turn him into dog food." At Sam's angry snort and nip at his ear, Jim slapped his neck fondly. "Don't worry, that'll never happen. We've been together too long, old pard." To Dave he continued. "Yep, feed and groomin' for Sam and Soot, my pardner's gray. We don't know how long we'll be in town, so keep them ready for us."

"I'll take good care of them," MacTavish promised the Rangers. "C'mon, you two." He took the reins of both horses, Sam now following meekly behind him.

❋   ❋   ❋

It was a restless night for the four lawmen as the anticipated reply from the Texas Northern didn't arrive, forcing them to wait for the telegraph office to reopen in the morning. Jim and Smoky spent most of the night dozing fitfully on the thin, lumpy mattresses in the jail cells. At seven they were already up, dressed, and sipping hot coffee with the marshal when Jeff Wehner knocked twice and strode inside.

"The Western Union'll be open any minute now. Let's head down there," he urged, not even bothering with a "Good Morning". "I'd sure like to get my hands on those blamed idiots in Dallas. We've lost an entire night already."

"We were just waitin' on you," Jim impatiently replied. "Let's go."

Moving at a brisk pace, it only took the foursome a couple of moments to reach the Western Union office in its small shack a block from the Graham railroad depot. As they swept into the cramped office, Henry Tombs jerked up his snowy head.

"Mr. Dobson, good morning. The same to you Marshal Wood, and you also, Rangers," Tombs smiled as he adjusted his spectacles.

"Morning, Henry," Wehner rather brusquely returned the elderly telegrapher's greeting. "Did I get a wire from Dallas yet?"

"You sure did. It came in overnight." Tombs pulled a yellow message flimsy from a pigeonhole, only to have Wehner fairly rip it from his grasp.

"Blast it!" The detective cursed as he quickly skimmed the telegram. "A train carrying a big gold shipment left Shreveport, Louisiana three days ago, and it's already pulled out of Dallas. We're too late to stop it."

"How about at Mineral Wells?" Jim asked. "Can we catch up to it there?"

"It's too late." Wehner shook his head in frustration. "We'd never make it in time ... although maybe I could get a man on the train there," he added thoughtfully. "However, that's a real long shot in any event."

"One man won't do a heckuva lot of good," Smoky observed as he took a long drag on his cigarette.

"No, but I figure those renegades, if they are gonna hit that train, won't pull the job until someplace further west," Wehner rejoined. "My guess is somewhere in the Palo Duros. There are plenty of places to run down a train there, while it's pulling some long grades. There's a water stop about twenty miles west of Mineral Wells. If we ride hard, we might catch the train there. Henry, wire this to the Texas Northern." He quickly dictated a message.

"Send one for us too, Henry," Jim ordered. "It goes to Captain Trumbull at Ranger Headquarters in Austin. With any luck there'll be a Ranger or two around Mineral Wells. The captain can order them onto that train."

"You want me to ride with you, Jim?" Brian asked as the telegrapher hunched over his clacking key.

"We'll be a long way out of your jurisdiction," Blawcyzk replied.

"Yeah Jim, but we'll need every gun we can get if those hombres hit that train," Smoky pointed out.

"Your partner's right, Lieutenant," Wehner agreed. "And I can solve that problem. Marshal Brian Wood, I hereby swear you in as a special agent of the Texas Northern Railroad. Now let's get the horses!" The detective bulled his way out of the tiny telegraph office with the others at his heels as he hustled up the dusty street toward the livery stable. Less than fifteen minutes later, the quartet of lawmen pounded out of Graham.

CHAPTER 14

"Blast it, we're too late!" Wood exclaimed as early the next morning they topped a ridge within view of the water stop, which was still a good mile off. The train was just pulling away from the tower, the locomotive's black smoke staining the clear blue Texas sky. The lawmen had pushed their horses hard all the previous day and night, but Jim's paint and Smoky's steeldust were still tired from their exertions of the past several days, while Wood's grulla and the big buckskin Wehner rode were unable to match the pace of the Rangers' tough, speedy mounts, even with Sam and Soot's worn-out condition. The rugged cross-country run had taken longer than the Rangers had wanted.

"Not yet we're not!" Blawcyzk firmly stated. "We'll catch that train at the upgrade Jeff talked about, on the other side of that rise." During their ride Wehner had described a spot where he felt the outlaws might hit the train ... a long climb through a deep cut, past sight of the water stop, where the train would slow as the engine struggled up the grade. Jim pushed Sam into a dead run, with Smoky and Soot right at his heels. Wood and Wehner exhorted their mounts to follow as best they could.

The Rangers swiftly closed the gap while the train started its long climb, slowing for the first rise, gaining speed as the tracks momentarily leveled off, then its momentum slackening considerably as it hit the long upgrade. Jim and Smoky urged their horses up close next to the slowing cars.

One of the outlaws already in place on the train spotted the pursuing Rangers, badges glinting on their chests. Slamming open a window, he wildly emptied his pistol in their direction. Lead whined wickedly past Jim and Smoky as they raced alongside the train, which consisted of the engine and its tender, an express car, three passenger coaches, several boxcars, and a caboose.

Smoky dove from his saddle and rolled onto the caboose's platform, while Jim lunged for the ladder at the front of the first boxcar, just behind the passenger coaches. Jim grabbed a rung, letting the train's momentum pull him from Sam's back, and hung swaying by one hand as his feet sought purchase on the lower rungs. The gunman in the rearmost coach had ducked back inside to reload and now reappeared, leaning far out of the window to take careful aim at Blawcyzk and pull the trigger. Jim's boot toe caught a rung and his free hand grasped desperately for his Colt as the slug burned a hot streak across his back. While blood trickled inside his shirt, Jim yanked the heavy Peacemaker from its holster, leaned back, and fired across his middle. His bullet caught the gunman square in the chest, its impact slamming the outlaw back against the window, cracking it. As the dying renegade sagged over the sill, the jarred-loose window dropped, pinning him. Slipping his pistol back into its holster and shaking off the effects of the bullet burn on his back, Jim swung from the ladder and onto the coach platform.

"What the devil is going on?" Major Thaddeus Saunders shouted. At the sound of the shots he had leapt from his seat to glare angrily out his window in the middle coach. "Who are those men?" His confederates were already on their feet, each now holding a revolver on the shocked passengers.

"They look like Rangers to me, sir," Sergeant Jeremiah Duffy calmly answered as he pulled his head back inside. "We can take care of them without too much trouble."

"See to it, Duffy," Saunders ordered, "And tell Morton and Ronson to get the coaches uncoupled. Brady, guard this car." Saunders turned to warn the passengers, "We'll be leaving you now. Anyone who makes a move will be cut down as soon as he comes through that door." Drawing his own pistol the major urged, "Hurry, Duffy, we'll have to move quickly." Leaving Brady with his gun still leveled at the now utterly terrified passengers, Saunders and Duffy hurried forward toward the express car.

Smoky climbed to the caboose roof, intending to make his way along the roofs of the cars then down into the engine's cab. With any luck he and Jim would be able to pin the train robbers in a crossfire.

Crouched low, Smoky scrambled across the swaying tops of the freight cars, fighting to keep his balance against the rocking of the train. Thick black smoke, filled with cinders, blew back from the locomotive's diamond stack, forcing him to keep his head ducked low between his shoulders. The wind had already ripped his Stetson from his head and now ruffled his thick black, silver tipped hair.

As Smoky jumped the gap between the first boxcar and the rearmost coach, the train jolted on a rough section of track. He landed hard on all fours, nearly going over the side, and curled up silently cursing the blinding pain in his knees. Recovering, he lifted his head to see two men on the roof of the foremost coach, heading back down the train in his direction. The Ranger and the two outlaws yelped in simultaneous surprise.

One of the robbers ran back to the head of the coach and disappeared down the ladder. The other pulled a gun and started blazing away at McCue. Smoky returned his fire, but aiming was impossible atop the rocking cars, and neither man scored a hit.

The locomotive whistle sounded, shrill and urgent. Smoky aimed one last quick shot and dropped spread-eagled on the roof. Too late, Corporal Stuart Morton sensed an onrushing presence behind him, turning to look just as the train entered a tunnel through a section of cap rock. Morton was smashed against the rock wall above the tunnel entrance, then his body was swept off the coach to lie broken and mangled just inside the tunnel.

Smoky clung desperately to the boxcar roof, fighting the thick smoke that clogged his lungs. After what seemed an eternity the train finally emerged from the tunnel. Smoky gasped frantically for fresh air as he felt the savage burn of cinders in his throat. He ran a hand across his smarting, watering eyes, fighting desperately to clear his vision, and began slowly crawling ahead to where the other gunman had disappeared.

Smoky leapt across to the roof of the lead coach just as the grade began leveling off slightly and the gap between coach and express car seemed to widen somewhat when the train began to pick up speed. Scrambling to his feet, the Ranger dashed recklessly ahead. Eyes still swimming, he peered down to see Private Pete Ronson perched precariously on the express car platform, pulling the pin from the coupler.

McCue fired almost blindly at the blurred figure below. Ronson gave a startled yelp of pain and surprise as the Ranger's .45 slug blasted downward through his shoulder. With the shock of the bullet's impact Ronson lost his grip on the railing and slipped under the cars. His scream of terror was cut short as he disappeared beneath the train.

Ronson had succeeded in pulling the pin more than halfway from the coupling drawhead before Smoky's bullet had cut him down. Now as the train rocked over an uneven section of roadbed the pin threatened to work its way loose entirely and separate the following cars from the rest of the train. As the couplers slammed back and forth, Smoky scrambled down the ladder then stepped onto the adjoining couplers, perilously balanced as he grasped the eye of the coupling pin. Every muscle straining with the effort, the Ranger finally managed to bring the pin back upright and slam it back into place. Smoky grabbed the railing of the express car and shakily pulled himself onto the platform. With a gusty sigh of relief, he leaned against the car wall as he pulled the kerchief from around his neck to wipe his sweat-soaked brow.

"I sure could use a smoke and a drink," Smoky muttered as he shakily reloaded his sixgun. "But I guess they'll have to wait until we're finished here."

❈   ❈   ❈

Jim had come through the back door of the rearmost passenger coach and now stood in the aisle, crouched low with his gun at the ready. Several of the car's petrified passengers pointed silently forward. Jim raced through the coach, leapt the gap to the next car, and had walked halfway up its aisle when Trooper Brady rose from behind a seat to level his gun at the Ranger. Jim had just begun to thumb back the hammer of his Colt when the train lurched and he was thrown off balance, the gun falling from his hand and spinning out of reach as he went to his knees. Brady took slow, deliberate aim at Jim's chest.

As he pulled back the hammer of his pistol, Brady's eyes widened in sudden astonishment. Braced for the impact of hot lead ripping through his body, Jim could only stare as blood welled from the soldier's mouth and nose and the gun dropped from his hand. Soundlessly Brady pitched forward on his face with a huge Bowie knife buried to its hilt in the middle of his back.

"It's about time you got here, Jim," a familiar voice chided.

"Rudy! Where'd you come from?" Jim asked in bewilderment as Ranger Rudy Flores rose from his seat, dropping the poncho that had concealed his knife.

"Captain Trumbull got your wire. But let's worry about that later," Flores replied as he coolly pulled his Bowie from the dead Brady's back and pointed it toward a window. "It seems like we've got more company on the way." Even as Flores spoke a bullet shattered the window next to him, whistling past his head to bury itself in the coach wall.

"You take care of 'em, Rudy," Jim ordered, "I'm goin' after the head honchos." As Rudy pulled out his Colt and began blazing away at the approaching riders, Jim retrieved his own pistol, then headed for the foremost coach.

❦   ❦   ❦

Lead whistled around Smoky McCue, pinning him to the floor of the express car's platform. The remainder of Saunders' men realized things had gone awry as the train they were intending to loot sped past them without stopping. The blue-uniformed riders kicked their horses into frantic pursuit, intending to overwhelm by sheer numbers whoever was trying to ruin their plan.

Lying flat on his belly, Smoky managed to pick off two of the approaching raiders, waiting until they were almost upon him to blast them from their saddles. He drilled another with a bullet through the shoulder, causing the man to drop his reins as he slumped over his horse's neck and rode out of the fray. Meanwhile Rudy, crouched by the coach window, steadied his gun on the windowsill to carefully aim at a shouting rider as the man stretched out to reach for a boxcar's ladder. He fired and dispatched the renegade cavalryman with a bullet through the stomach. His gun now empty, Rudy dropped away from the window as he reloaded. Easing back into position, he saw another soldier leap for the coach, only to be killed in mid-air as Smoky put a bullet into his back.

While the fight raged, Jim paused on the middle coach's forward platform to reload, then pushed his way into the first coach. Major Saunders and Sergeant Duffy whirled with drawn guns to face the coldly determined Ranger.

"Texas Rangers! You're under arrest!" Blawcyzk calmly stated, his voice low and menacing.

"I hardly think so," Saunders snarled as without a word Duffy leveled his pistol at the Ranger's middle. Before the sergeant could thumb back the hammer Jim fired his own Colt, the bullet slamming into Duffy's chest just under the left shirt pocket and spinning him half-around. Duffy grunted as the slug tore into him, crumpled onto an empty seat, then slipped to the floor.

As Duffy went down, Saunders yanked his saber from its scabbard and lunged at Blawcyzk. Reacting instantly, Jim triggered his sixgun again, but was foiled by the rocking of the train, which was now gathering even more speed on the downgrade as the engineer desperately attempted to outrun the outlaws. The bullet went wide of its mark and Saunders slashed out with his saber, ripping Jim's shirt across the chest and opening a long slash across his right breast, angling downward across the Ranger's chest and stomach. Blood ran freely from the jagged wound, mixing with the sweat matting the thick blonde hair on Blawcyzk's chest and belly.

As Jim stumbled backwards in pain and shock, Saunders sneered in triumph as he drew back his saber to drive it through the Ranger's belly. Jim barely sidestepped in time to catch the flat of the thrusting blade between his right arm and side, pinning it. He jabbed the barrel of his Peacemaker into the pit of the major's stomach and pulled the trigger.

As the bullet tore through him Saunders sagged back, but his eyes still held their malevolent gleam and his hand still tightly gripped the handle of his saber. As he took one staggering step toward Blawcyzk, Jim lifted the muzzle of his pistol slightly and fired again, this bullet slamming into the middle of Saunders' chest and through his heart. The renegade major was smashed back against the bulkhead of the coach by the impact of the point-blank slug. With a final defiant curse, Saunders slid down the wall, then toppled sideways to the floor.

Blawcyzk sagged against a blood-splattered bench just as Smoky burst through the door and rushed up to him.

"Jim! Are you okay?" Smoky shouted, his eyes widening at the blood running down his partner's chest, Blawcyzk's ripped-open shirt revealing the vicious slash across his upper torso.

"Yeah … I'll be … okay, Smoke," Jim nodded, gasping. "Rudy's somewhere on this train too." As if on cue the rear door of the coach quietly opened and Rudy Flores appeared, a still-smoking Colt in his hand.

"Jim?" Flores took in the gruesome scene before him.

"I'll be … fine, Rudy. Just let me … rest a couple of minutes." Jim's breathing was heavy, his eyes glassy with pain, and he swayed drunkenly with the train's motion. Smoky watched him closely while Rudy scanned the passengers for any possum playing robbers. As the rails clicked hypnotically below, Jim suddenly jerked his head up and his eyes became focused.

"Hey, one of you get the engineer to stop this thing," he ordered. "We've got to round up Brian and Jeff."

CHAPTER 15

With a soft groan Jim slumped across the bench, his gun loose in his fingers. Smoky leaned worriedly over his partner, looking fearfully at the copiously bleeding saber wound slicing across Blawcyzk's chest and stomach.

"Smoky, I'll get the engineer to stop," Flores flatly stated. "You get Jim patched up." Blood dripped from a bullet slash above Rudy's left ear, and a crimson stain on the right side of his shirt indicated where a slug had torn along his ribs.

A fortyish matron in the seat behind Blawcyzk and McCue calmly told Smoky, "Ranger, I have an extra petticoat in my traveling bag. I'll help you care for your partner." She stood up and removed a battered blue and red carpetbag from the overhead shelf.

"Thank you, ma'am. I'm obliged," Smoky answered as he pulled off Jim's torn, blood-soaked shirt.

"That goes for me as well, ma'am," Jim weakly answered. His blue eyes were now glazed with pain.

"Anything I can do to help, Rangers. My word, what was all that about?" the woman questioned. Now that the shooting had stopped and Saunders and his men were lying dead or wounded on the coach floors or scattered back along the tracks, several of the male passengers came forward to offer the Rangers assistance.

"Those hombres that have been raiding the stages and raillines took on this train. We almost beat 'em to it," Smoky briefly explained, his calloused fingers surprisingly gentle as he deftly pushed together the edges of the saber slash across Jim's chest and stomach. As with most Rangers, necessity had made Smoky fairly proficient at rough frontier doctoring. While he worked on his partner's wound he glanced up at the hovering men and suggested, "You might want to get those bodies out of the way for now."

"Here, Ranger. I'm Nancy Cochran, by the way." The buxom matron had ripped several strips from a clean petticoat and now handed them to Smoky, then helped him lift Jim's shoulders so he could bind the wound tightly.

"Well, I sure appreciate your help, ma'am," Smoky gratefully replied. "I'm Smoky McCue, and my pard here's Jim Blawcyzk. I must say you've been mighty brave about this, Miz Cochran."

"Mercy sakes, this is nothing," Nancy declared. "My husband Barry and I fought the Comanches for years after we settled in Texas. And we even managed to have a boy and a girl while those Indians were still prowling around. However, I must admit you boys did put on quite a show today." She smiled as she propped Jim against the seat back while Smoky finished bandaging his chest.

"There Jim. That's the best I can do for now," Smoky said as he straightened up.

"It feels pretty good, Smoke. Thanks," Jim answered as he struggled to sit up.

"Hey! Where do you think you're goin', pardner? You don't want to bust yourself wide open again," Smoky cautioned.

"We're not finished yet. We've still got to find Brian and Jeff and round up our horses." Jim stared at his partner for a minute, then started chuckling uncontrollably.

"What the devil's so funny, Blawcyzk?" Smoky growled.

"Just you." Jim paused for a moment to catch his breath. McCue was black from head to toe, covered with soot and cinders from the locomotive's smokestack. "You look just like your name, pard ... Smoky!"

"That's not funny, Jim," Smoky grumbled.

"I'm afraid your partner is right." Nancy Cochran giggled, then began laughing uproariously when the rest of the passengers joined in, as much from suddenly relieved tension as the hilarity of Jim's comment.

"It's still not that funny," Smoky repeated.

"Smoke, you could always tell me your real name," Jim pointed out.

"And like I've told you before Jim, if I ever did I'd have to gutshoot you," Smoky retorted. "C'mon, let's get you settled, then I'll see if Rudy needs any help." The train was now noticeably losing speed.

"When you find him, tell him to have the engineer back this thing up," Jim ordered, wiping tears of laughter from his eyes. "We've got to find Jeff and Brian and our horses."

"Sure, Jim." Knowing his partner as he did, Smoky was certain Jim was as concerned about the fate of their mounts as those of the railroad detective and marshal, maybe even more so.

❦   ❦   ❦

Rudy had no difficulty convincing the engineer to stop once he finally got past the express car. The guards inside, under strict orders not to open that car for anyone, at first refused to let the swarthy Texican pass through the car. Rudy then considered the roof, but quickly discarded the idea when he realized such a move would most likely get him blasted off the train by a shotgun load of buckshot. Instead he kept arguing with the rightfully dubious guards. Finally convinced by the badge Flores wore as well as the outlaws they'd seen shot from their horses, the two express messengers warily opened the reinforced door. The leveled muzzles of their shotguns never left Rudy's belly until he was out the other door and climbing onto the tender. Rudy knew the guards would have cut him down instantly at the slightest false move, and at that range their buckshot would have cut him to ribbons. The guards eased back a bit as the train slowed, and a few moments later when Smoky entered the car they were visibly relieved.

"Those hombres taken care of, Ranger?" one of the guards, youthful and sporting a wispy mustache, asked in a shaky voice, still clutching his double-barreled Greener.

"It looks like it. Just keep an eye peeled for stragglers," McCue ordered as he headed for the engine's cab, where Rudy had already convinced the crew to stop the train.

Flores whirled at the sound of someone behind him, instinctively reaching for his pistol as Smoky jumped down from the tender. He relaxed as he recognized his partner.

"Smoky, is Jim gonna be all right?" he questioned as he slid the gun back into its holster.

"I've got to say I'm afraid so, Rudy." Smoky ruefully shook his head. "The lieutenant's givin' orders already, as usual." He turned to the gray-bearded engineer and gangly teenaged fireman. "Our boss wants you to back this train up to the water stop. If you see any horses or riders along the way make sure you stop for them. We've got a couple of pardners following us."

"With pleasure, Ranger," the engineer readily agreed, his relief plain in his voice and evident all over his countenance. He shoved the throttle into reverse, released the brake, and the young fireman resumed his steady shoveling rhythm. The train headed uphill, slowly at first, then gradually building speed as it crested the summit.

"Shouldn't you slow this thing down a bit, Mister?" Smoky anxiously asked as the train gained momentum on the downslope, the cars tilting and swaying as they rounded several curves.

"I was just gettin' ready to do that, Ranger," the engineer answered as he eased off on the throttle and partially engaged the brake. "There. That better?" he grinned as the train slowed considerably.

"Much," Smoky agreed. "And don't forget to keep an eye peeled for our pards."

"Of course," the engineer reassured him. "I haven't forgotten about 'em."

The train continued to roll back downgrade, soon reaching the level, straight stretch between the cut and the water stop. Before long Smoky shouted for the engineer to halt as he spied Jeff Wehner and Brian Wood alongside the rails. Several men in cavalry uniforms, their hands tied, stood sullenly under the watchful eyes and steady rifles of the lawmen.

And to Smoky's great relief Soot and Sam were peacefully grazing a short way off, along with Brian's grulla and Jeff's buckskin.

Jim had managed to stumble out of the lead coach even before the train had come to a complete stop and Smoky and Rudy had swung down from the locomotive's cab.

"Jeff! Brian!" he exclaimed as he stepped down to the roadbed. Hearing Jim's voice, Sam lifted his head and whickered to his friend. Jim smiled and called out, "I'll be with you in a bit, pal." To Jeff and Brian he continued, "I see you rounded up a few."

"We sure did," Wehner replied, "And as we guessed they're regular Army, under the command of a Major Thaddeus Saunders." High on the right shoulder of the detective's shirt was a spreading crimson stain, while Wood's left arm hung limp in a makeshift sling, the forearm shattered by a rifle slug. A bandanna wrapped around the marshal's right leg soaked up blood oozing from a bullet tear in his thigh.

"Well, Saunders won't be commanding anyone except those hombres shoveling coal into Hell's furnaces," Smoky dryly remarked as he strode up.

"It looks like you've already been down there," Brian laughed as he appraised the soot-streaked Ranger.

"Not you too, Wood," Smoky growled.

"Yeah, and how come you're the only one of us who didn't catch a slug, Smoky?" Wehner challenged as he gazed at the bandages wrapped around Jim's chest. "And who's your friend?" He nodded toward Rudy, who was making his way back along the train.

"That's Ranger Rudy Flores," Jim explained, greeting Sam with a fond slap on the neck as the paint trotted up to him and nuzzled his shoulder. "Captain Trumbull got our wire, and got a message through to Rudy in time to get him on board." Glancing at McCue he continued, "Yeah, Smoke. How'd you miss takin' a bullet, when the rest of us got shot up?"

"These renegades didn't want to mess up my handsome face," Smoky retorted. The others responded to his smirk with groans of disbelief.

"Well what now, Jim?" Brian asked, getting back to business. "Are we haulin' these hombres back to my jail?"

Blawcyzk shook his head as peeled off his torn shirt, tossed it aside, and dug in his saddlebags for a clean one. "What you do with the train and the money is your decision, Jeff," he told Wehner. "But these men are in Ranger custody, and we'll be taking them back to Fort Griffin, Marshal," he said in answer to Wood's question. "I imagine Colonel Thomas will have plans for a court martial. If he doesn't, then we'll bring charges against 'em in the circuit court."

CHAPTER 16

"In spite of everything you've told me, even now I find it extremely difficult to believe Thaddeus Saunders convinced an entire company of his troopers to go along with this infernal scheme," Colonel Lyndall Thomas flatly declared over a puff of smoke from the huge cigar he held clamped between his teeth. His dark eyes still held a flat challenge as he gazed at Blawcyzk. "I would have thought at least one man, if not several, would have revealed his plans to myself or another officer."

The Rangers had returned with their prisoners to Fort Griffin, where the captives were now safely ensconced in the post stockade. The bodies of Major Saunders, Sergeant Duffy, and the rest of the outlaw soldiers killed in the aborted train robbery had also been returned to the fort where they would be discreetly buried, without ceremony or military honors, in the post cemetery. Jeff Wehner had wired that the gold shipment was safely at its destination, while Brian Wood was back at his office in Graham, his wounded arm in a sling. He would have to decide fairly quickly who he could hire as a deputy until he recovered from his wounds sufficiently to return fully to his duties. Jim, Smoky, and Rudy had spent the last three hours briefing Thomas on what had transpired the past few days.

"At least a couple of them did try Colonel, from what we've learned," Jim answered, "but Saunders had them murdered, then reported to you that they had died in the line of duty while fighting Comanches. And at least one man, Private Luis Rivera, was killed by a stagecoach shotgun guard." Still uncomfortably bandaged around his torso, Jim twisted around in his chair. "However, the clincher was that information you provided before Smoky and I left here. Every robbery coincided with the times Saunders and his men were out on patrol. While they were here at the fort, not one person, stage, or train was held up."

"It's still hard to believe," Thomas muttered, shaking his head in disbelief. "A career officer with a service record as fine as Major Saunders' …" His voice trailed off in dejection. The colonel took another puff on his cigar before continuing.

"Lieutenant Blawcyzk, Corporal McCue, I would like to apologize for the reception I gave you when you first arrived here in Fort Griffin."

"There's no apology necessary, Colonel," Jim easily replied. "We both kind of got off on the wrong foot that day. And I can certainly understand why you were reluctant to think any soldiers under your command would be involved in wholesale robbery and murder. I'd have the same problem believing that about any of the men I've served with in the Texas Rangers."

"I don't know about that," Thomas suddenly grinned as he gazed at Smoky McCue, who was tipped back in a chair in the corner where he was happily puffing away on one of the colonel's expensive cigars. "Your partner there certainly was quick enough about stealing one of my cheroots."

"I prefer the term 'borrowed', Colonel." Smoky chuckled as he took a sip of bourbon from the glass in his hand. "And this is real fine whiskey you've got here too."

"Colonel, any time you want to press charges against my pard, I'll be happy to oblige you," Jim laughed. "In fact we could have a court martial right now."

"I don't think that will be necessary," Thomas smiled. "However, speaking of that, I would request you remain here for the courts-martial of those men if at all possible. We will require your testimony."

"That shouldn't be a problem, at least for Smoky and myself. I'll wire Captain Trumbull just to make sure he doesn't have anything else planned for us," Jim replied, then took a long drink of water from the cut-crystal tumbler he held. His gaze then turned to Rudy Flores, who was relaxing in a big leather chair in the corner opposite Smoky. Flores also held a glass of the colonel's aged bourbon and was smoking one of his expensive cigars.

"How about you, Rudy?" Jim asked. "Do you have to be back in Mineral Wells at any particular time?"

"Nope." Rudy grinned broadly as he replied. "Cap'n Trumbull turned me loose under your orders until Jim Huggins and some of the men from Company C get up here. Then I'm to ride with them."

"Sergeant Huggins is on his way up here?" Jim echoed.

"Yeah," Rudy confirmed. "With everything that's happened the past couple of days I plumb forgot to tell you that. He and the men riding with him will be stationed up here until things settle down in these parts. Once they arrive you and Smoky are to head back to Austin."

"Unless the courts-martial are still goin' on," Jim pointed out.

"I reckon that's so," Rudy concurred.

"So is everything settled?" Thomas queried.

"Seems to be, Colonel," Jim answered. "I'll wire Headquarters in the morning to let Captain Trumbull know we need to remain for the trials. But now I'd really like to get some rest, with your permission. It's been a rough couple of days."

"Not quite so fast," Thomas replied, looking at the faint thin ribbon of red apparent on Blawcyzk's shirtfront. The Ranger's wound was still oozing blood, which had seeped through the bandages Jim wore and the spare shirt he had donned back at the site of the train robbery. "I think you should see Doctor Gibson before you head back to your hotel and let him care for your wounds properly."

"There's no need for that," Jim protested. "Smoky did a decent job of patchin' me up. Once we get back to our room I'll clean up that cut and rebandage it. I'll be fine."

"The colonel's right, Jim," Smoky disagreed. "That's more'n just a cut you've got there. You're darn lucky Saunders didn't slice you wide open like a gutted catfish. You need to be stitched up."

"Don't bother arguing, Lieutenant," Rudy firmly added, his use of Jim's rank giving further emphasis to his words. "You're goin' to see the doc, and that's that." To Thomas he added, "Don't pay Jim any mind. He's generally a real easy-goin' hombre, but he's got a stubborn streak as wide as the Rio Grande."

"I can understand that," Thomas smiled. "So do I. Perhaps, Lieutenant Blawcyzk, that's the reason you and I didn't particularly like each other when we first met. But since I can be just as stubborn as you, you will go see Doctor Gibson before you're allowed off this post. Is that clear?"

"I can see all of you are gangin' up on me," Jim grumbled.

"That's right," Smoky retorted. "So let's not waste any more time."

"You win." Jim gave in with a sigh.

"Now you're making sense," Rudy said.

"Your men are right, and you know that," Thomas added. "So let Doctor Gibson treat you. Then get that night's rest, and we can finish our discussion in the morning ... say around ten."

"We'll see you then, Colonel," Smoky answered, before Jim could utter further protest. "Good night. C'mon, Jim, let's go." He and Rudy each grabbed the recalcitrant Blawcyzk by an arm to hustle him out of the office and across the compound to the post surgeon's office.

CHAPTER 17

"I'm just about finished with you, Lieutenant," Doctor David Gibson stated as he took the last stitch in Jim Blawcyzk's stomach. Jim was lying flat on his back on a table in the post hospital while the Army surgeon thoroughly cleaned out the saber slash across Jim's upper torso, trimmed away dead flesh from the edges, and was now stitching skin and muscle back together.

"I appreciate everything you've done, Doc," Jim gratefully said, wincing as Gibson spread a stinging salve over the wound, then taped a thick bandage in place.

"That goes for me too, Doc," Rudy Flores spoke up from his seat opposite the table. At Jim's insistence, Gibson had treated Rudy's relatively minor wounds before beginning work on Blawcyzk.

"You're both welcome," Gibson replied with a disbelieving shake of his head as he finished bandaging Jim. "And I must say you Rangers are every bit as tough as I'd heard. This saber slash you took would have incapacitated most men, Lieutenant ... and I'm including the soldiers of the United States Army."

"I couldn't let it stop me, or I would've been a goner," Jim explained. "That major was ready to shove his saber right through my guts. I had to get him first." He started to sit up.

"Not quite so fast, Lieutenant," Gibson objected. "I need you to roll over on your belly so I can treat that bullet burn on your back."

"That's nothing, Doc," Jim objected.

"Listen. You just let me be the doctor, and you stick to Rangering. Now roll onto your stomach," Gibson sternly ordered.

"Listen to the doc, Jim," Smoky McCue piped up from his chair next to Flores. "You tried to claim that "little" cut on your chest was nothing too … and it took what, thirty-seven stitches, Doc?"

"That's right, thirty-seven," Gibson confirmed.

"So stop being such a stubborn cuss and do as Doc Gibson says," Smoky concluded.

"All right." Reluctantly Jim complied, flipping onto his belly.

"This won't take long at all," Gibson noted with satisfaction as he studied the shallow gash across Jim's lower back. "Some medication and a bandage will do just fine. It won't need any stitches." Efficiently he dressed and bandaged the injury.

"There. You're all set for now, Lieutenant," the physician stated as he finished. "You can get redressed."

"You mean I can finally get out of here and get some sleep?" Jim answered.

"You can indeed, in fact I'd highly recommend it," Gibson answered as Jim swung his legs over the edge of the table, swaying only slightly as he came to his feet, then shrugged into his shirt. As Jim buckled his gunbelt back on, Gibson continued, "Now, you will need to come back in about ten days to have those stitches removed. And of course if you feel light-headed or feverish, get back here immediately. And don't plan on doing any riding or other strenuous activity for at least two or three weeks."

"Jim's always been kind of dizzy, so he'll have a hard time tellin' if he's light-headed, Doc." Smoky chortled.

"And he's already light-headed with that tow hair of his," Rudy added.

"Enough!" Gibson shouted. "Out of here, all of you."

"We're on our way," Jim answered as he tugged on his Stetson. "Good-bye, Doc."

❧   ❧   ❧

"I'm gonna check on Sam once more before I head back to the hotel," Jim told his partners as they left the post and began the short walk back to town. Smoky started to object but kept quiet, knowing he could never win an argument with Blawcyzk when it came to his horse.

"I reckon we'll come along with you and check our horses too," Rudy agreed. His palomino gelding Solana had been placed in a boxcar to be with his rider when Flores had boarded the train at Mineral Wells, and was now stabled at the only livery barn in Fort Griffin, along with Jim and Smoky's mounts.

"Suit yourselves, although I would think you'd have better things to do" Jim shrugged, not quite willing to admit he was actually grateful for the company.

As they reached what passed for the center of Fort Griffin, a shrill female voice rang out.

"Smoky! Smoky McCue!"

"Quick, hide me," Smoky pleaded in desperation at the sound of Cindy Lou's call. "Jim, Rudy … please." He looked around frantically for a storefront or alleyway to duck into and disappear.

"It's too late, pardner. She's got you cornered," Jim laughed as a very indignant Cindy Lou crossed the dusty street and stalked up to the trio of Rangers.

"Cindy Lou, darlin' …" Smoky weakly began.

"Don't you dare Cindy Lou me, Smoky McCue," the saloon girl huffed. "You told me you'd see me the night after we were together, and then you ride out without so much as a bye-your-leave."

"Cindy Lou. I had to. Duty called. You know I'm a Ranger. We had to leave town in a hurry," Smoky stammered. He shuffled awkwardly, glancing around at anywhere but Cindy's eyes. Jim and Rudy had never seen their partner quite so nervous.

"That's no excuse," Cindy insisted. "You could have stopped by for just a minute, and let me know. You … you …". Cindy's outburst was cut short as Smoky suddenly took her in his arms and crushed her lips to his. Even the jaded passersby of Fort Griffin stopped to stare at them.

"C'mon, Rudy," Jim chuckled. "Let's check on the horses, then I think I'd like to get a couple of drinks before turnin' in. These two need to be alone. See you in the mornin', Smoke." McCue didn't even appear to notice as his partners ambled off.

🍁   🍁   🍁

"Smoky?"

"Yes, Cindy honey?" The smoke-eyed Ranger sat on the edge of Cindy Lou's soft feather bed, his gunbelt off and lying on a chair, his Stetson, neckerchief, and shirt already shed. Cindy Lou was kneeling on the mattress behind him as she gently massaged his shoulders.

"I asked you the last time we were together what your real name is." Her nimble fingers deftly kneaded the nape of his neck, then her hands wandered lower as she began massaging the muscles of his back.

"And I told you then I don't tell that to anyone … for anything," Smoky gruffly replied.

"But you'll tell your Cindy Lou, won't you, Smoky?" she huskily purred. Her fingers worked their way over his ribs as she reached around to begin stroking his chest.

"Not even you, darlin'," Smoky gulped.

"Are you certain?" she leaned closer to whisper in his ear.

"I'm positive," Smoky insisted.

"Then you won't get another thing from me, Ranger McCue," Cindy firmly stated, pulling back from him.

"Cindy Lou, please," Smoky pleaded.

"I mean it, Mister," Cindy repeated, her eyes flashing angrily.

Smoky hesitated, his determination to maintain the secret he'd kept for years battling his desire for the attractive saloon woman. His blood was racing, pulse pounding, muscles tense with anticipation. Sweat glistened on his body as it oozed from every pore.

"Cindy," he entreated once more.

"Nothing, Smoky." To bedevil the Ranger further she ran a hand ever so slowly across his belly, just above his beltline. "Not unless you tell me your real name."

A soft groan escaped Smoky's lips. At that moment he would have preferred being smeared with honey and staked out on an ant hill by Comanches to being in this spot.

"You win," he finally conceded as his face flushed with embarrassment, "It's … Barnabas," he grudgingly admitted.

"Barnabas?" Cindy Lou drew back, her eyes filled with mirth and a delighted smile playing across her lips.

Smoky nodded glumly. "That's it. Barnabas. Now are you satisfied?"

"Why that's a lovely name," Cindy Lou declared with conviction, "And I promise never to call you Barney, you big ol' lug."

"Never mind about that," Smoky dejectedly answered. "Just promise me never, and I mean never, to tell anyone else … especially Jim. He'd never let me live it down."

"Jim!" Cindy Lou snorted disdainfully. "He's just an old stick in the mud who won't even drink with a lady. But I won't tell him, I promise … Barnabas."

"Please, can't you just keep callin' me Smoky, Cindy Lou?" McCue begged.

"In another minute, you won't care *what* I call you, Ranger," Cindy Lou retorted, as she wrapped her arms around him.

CHAPTER 18

❀

Captain Trumbull readily gave his permission for Blawcyzk, McCue, and Flores to remain at Fort Griffin and testify at the courts-martial of the surviving members of Major Saunders' renegade band of cavalry soldiers. In addition, the captain further ordered them to remain in Fort Griffin until the arrival of Sergeant Jim Huggins and his group of hand-picked Rangers from Company C.

Smoky and Rudy went out on some routine patrols while waiting for the Army trials to begin, and in the course of those made several arrests. Jim, unable to ride due to his wounds, spent the time caring for Sam or lazing in a chair in front of the hotel, soaking up the sunshine, chafing with impatience and becoming more frustrated at being laid up with each passing day. By the time the courts-martial began, Jim was champing at the bit to be back in the saddle.

With the testimony of the Rangers, Detective Wehner of the Texas Northern Railroad and Marshal Wood of Graham, along with that of several of the passengers from the last attempted train robbery, the outcome of the trials was a foregone conclusion.

Under oath, Corporal Sam Grestini related Major Thaddeus Saunders' reason for turning outlaw.

"The major needed lots of money because he wanted to stake a big claim down along the Mexican border," the cleanshaven young corporal explained to the spectators in the hushed chamber, as he sat with his back ramrod straight and his eyes staring straight ahead. "He said there'd be a place for each of us, and a good-sized share of some real big profits."

"Profits from what?" Captain Robert Steele, the prosecutor from the judge advocate general's office, queried.

"Running guns, moving stolen cattle, smuggling all sorts of contraband across the border … in both directions," Grestini clarified. "Our jobs would be to guard and hold this ford across the Rio Grande which the major had scouted out. He said it was the best crossing for a hundred miles in all directions, and it was right in line with a hidden pass up into the Balcones. He claimed the spot was made to order for smuggling, and there'd be plenty of money in it for all of us."

Colonel Thomas looked across the courtroom from where he sat behind a table, idly turning a stub of pencil in his hands. When he caught Blawcyzk's gaze, he shook his head slightly as he pursed his lips. Almost imperceptibly Jim nodded at Thomas. He and the colonel evidently had the same thought, that it was far more likely once Major Saunders had amassed sufficient wealth he would have disposed of most, if not all, of the men he'd duped into following him and disappear into Mexico, or perhaps even somewhere in South America. Obviously Saunders had never had any intention of retiring on the small income a government pension would provide.

"Thank you, Corporal. That will be all," Steele softly answered as Grestini concluded his testimony.

❦   ❦   ❦

With the overwhelming evidence against them, none of the convicted men chose to appeal the guilty verdicts they received. Due to the enormity of their crimes, the judges of the military tribunal who had conducted the courts-martial sentenced each man to death by firing squad. One week after the trial, under a steady rain that turned Fort Griffin's parade ground into a muddy quagmire, the sentences were carried out.

CHAPTER 19

❀

Three days after the trial, a wire from Captain Trumbull at Ranger Headquarters was received at the fort's telegraph office. Colonel Thomas himself brought it to the Rangers at their hotel. He found the three lawmen relaxing in tipped-back chairs in front of the building, their booted feet up on the hitchrail. Jim was dozing, his Stetson pulled low over his eyes, while Smoky was puffing on one of his endless quirlies and Rudy was munching on some jerky and leftover biscuits.

"Good morning, men," Thomas cordially greeted them.

"Mornin', Colonel," Jim replied for all three as he thumbed back his hat and dropped his feet to the boardwalk. "What brings you by on this fine, sunny day?" After several days of thick humidity and off and on thunderstorms, the morning had finally dawned bright and clear, with a refreshing northerly breeze.

"A telegram arrived for you sometime overnight," Thomas explained. "I thought I would deliver it to you personally, since if the message is what I suspect this may well be my last chance to visit with you." He handed the yellow message flimsy to Jim, who quickly perused its contents.

"Well Jim, what's it say?" Smoky impatiently demanded.

"Jim Huggins and five men from Company C will be arriving here at Fort Griffin within the next couple of days. They'll be patrolling this entire section of the state for the next several months," Jim answered.

"It must say more than that, Jim," Rudy insisted.

"It does," Jim conceded. "Once Huggins gets here Smoky and I will be riding out."

"I think perhaps your partner would like to know where you're headed, Lieutenant," Colonel Thomas pointed out.

"The colonel's right, Jim," Smoky confirmed. "So stop dawdling. Where are we goin'?"

Jim grinned broadly as he answered, "We'll be heading back to Austin for now. It looks like we'll be getting a few days to spend at home, then we'll receive orders."

"That's the best news I've heard in a month of Sundays," Smoky whooped. "There's a little gal I met at the Silver Star who ... on second thought, never mind," he concluded.

"Well, since you'll be here at Fort Griffin for at least a few more days after all, I'd like to take this opportunity to invite you to the post for a farewell supper before you leave, gentlemen," Colonel Thomas invited. "Would tomorrow evening be suitable?"

"Gee, I dunno." Jim thoughtfully rubbed his jaw. "All those fancy drinks and rich food, extravagant pastries for dessert, all set on fine china and clean linens. And no bacon and beans ..."

"We accept with pleasure, Colonel," Smoky broke in as he thumped Jim on the arm. "Kindly ignore my thick-headed partner here."

"Of course," Thomas chuckled. "Tomorrow evening at eight. Good day, men." He touched the brim of his campaign hat in a brief salute, then turned on his heels, mounted his tall bay gelding, and trotted the horse briskly out of town.

CHAPTER 20

"Well, it's gonna be a shame havin' to eat Jim's cooking after that fine meal Colonel Thomas put on for us last night," Smoky remarked as late the next morning they left the Fort Griffin General Store. He and Blawcyzk had stopped at the mercantile to resupply for their long journey back to Austin. Jim had as usual cleaned out the entire stock of peppermints to make sure he would not run short of Sam's favorite treat on the trail, while Smoky had purchased enough tobacco and cigarette papers to assure he would have sufficient smokes until they reached their destination. Uncharacteristically, all three of the Rangers had slept until midmorning, tired from the late hour at which the farewell banquet had concluded and the tremendous amount of food they'd consumed. In addition, Smoky and Rudy were still slightly the worse for wear from the rounds of whiskey and liqueurs they'd imbibed. To add to their feeling of indolence, a heavy rainfall that had begun while they were at supper settled into a steady light drizzle which had continued all night, so the morning had dawned dank and gloomy. The sun was just now burning through the low clouds.

"You'll have to put up with his grub, Smoke but I won't, since I'll be remaining here in Fort Griffin," Rudy pointed out as they paused on the edge of the sidewalk and he shifted the sack in his hands.

"Nobody's forcin' either one of you to eat my chuck," Jim grumbled. "You can always go hungry."

"That might be preferable to the bellyaches I get from your biscuits," Smoky rejoined then stopped short, looking around in near panic.

"Oh Lord no!" he exclaimed when he caught sight of Cindy Lou as she emerged from Wetmore's Café and headed in the Rangers' direction. It only took her a moment to close the distance between them and stalk up to McCue, her eyes reflecting hurt and disappointment.

"You won't change your mind, Smoky?" the saloon girl questioned.

"Cindy, I'm a Texas Ranger. I have to go where I'm sent. I explained all that to you," Smoky quietly replied.

"But what about me? I thought …" Cindy Lou's voice faltered, her gaze dropping. "I thought we had something special."

"We did, Cindy Lou," Smoky answered, "But I have to be movin' on. Besides, I'm sure you won't be lonesome."

Cindy's eyes widened in anger. "Smoky McCue … you … you …" Furiously she slammed both hands against his chest. As he was rocked back by the unexpected blow, Smoky's boot heel caught in a crack in the rough boardwalk, sending him sprawling backward into the muddy street. The horrible crack of a breaking bone echoed audibly across the street. Smoky tried to push himself up, then fell back, grimacing with pain as his leg collapsed under him.

"Oh, *Barnabas!*" Cindy Lou screeched as she clamped her hands to her mouth in horror. "What have I done to you?" Wailing, she hurried from the walk to kneel in the muck alongside Smoky. "I didn't mean to hurt you."

"Just … just what did you call me?" Smoky snapped, as realization set in. The pain flushing his face was now supplanted by embarrassment and anger.

"She called you Barnabas, pardner," Jim laughed. "Don't tell me *that's* your real name, McCue." Beside him, Rudy trembled as he tried with only partial success to contain his mirth.

"Smoky. Oh, no. I didn't mean to," Cindy whimpered. "It's just that when I saw you hurt it … it slipped out."

"Cindy." McCue shook his head in disbelief, struck speechless.

Barnabas! No wonder you didn't want anyone to know your name, Smoke." Tears were rolling down Jim's cheeks as he doubled over with laughter. Almost overcome with hilarity, the lanky Ranger swayed precariously at the edge of the boardwalk. Too late, he tried to pull back as his foot slipped off the edge and he overbalanced and toppled forward. A hitchrail caught him just above the belt buckle and his laughter was momentarily choked off as the air was driven from his lungs. He jackknifed over the rail and somersaulted into the road, landing on his back in the mud with a huge splat.

"Serves you right, Jim," McCue growled as he scooped up a thick gob of mud. Ignoring the pain shooting through his broken leg, he let the mud fly, catching Blawcyzk square in the face.

"Oh yeah, *Barnabas?*" Jim chortled, grabbing a handful of sticky muck and letting it go, splattering it into Smoky's chest.

"Try that again, Jim. I dare you." Smoky challenged, as he gathered another fistful of glop. Within moments, both partners were covered head to toe with mud. Then their laughter slowed, and in sudden silence they stared up at the boardwalk where an untouched Rudy was still convulsed with laughter.

"Oh no you don't," Flores yelped as he instantly grasped his partners' intentions.

"Oh yeah we do," Jim grinned as Rudy pivoted to dive for cover inside the store. Before Flores could reach shelter, Jim sent an enormous blob of muck smacking into his back, then Rudy was pinned against the wall under a veritable barrage of mud. He sank to the walk, laughing wildly.

"Stop it, all of you!" Cindy Lou shrieked from where she'd fled, several feet away.

Jim and Smoky glanced at each other in complete understanding.

"Her turn!" Jim fired first, his aim unintentionally truer than he'd intended, as the huge glob of mud landed right smack in the middle of Cindy Lou's cleavage to dribble down between her full breasts. As much from surprise as the impact, Cindy sat down hard in the middle of a puddle. When she did Jim and Smoky, laughing uncontrollably, slathered her with mud.

Smoky had just picked up another handful of muck to toss in Cindy's direction when he stopped short to gaze at a column of men and horses approaching at a lope. A moment later the column came to a halt alongside the mud smeared trio.

"Lieutenant, I realize it's not Saturday night, but you sure could use a bath there. I reckon that goes for all of you." Texas Ranger Sergeant Jim Huggins grinned down from the back of his leggy chestnut gelding, Dusty. "You want to explain to me what's goin' on here?"

"You might want to ask Barnabas that, Jim," Blawcyzk replied, with a nod in Smoky's direction.

"You mean that's McCue's real name?" Huggins drawled. "Why, that's a fine old Christian name. Goes all the way back to the Apostles."

"So there, Jim," Smoky retorted.

"It might be a fine old name, but it still sounds awful funny on you, pard," Jim answered. "I reckon I'll stick with callin' you Smoky."

"If y'all are through playin' in the muck, me and the boys would sure like you to show us a place to rest up and get some grub," Huggins dryly stated. "And who's your lady friend?"

"They're no friends of mine, Ranger!" Cindy Lou huffed.

"Don't believe a word she's sayin', Sergeant," Smoky retorted. "Even if she did break my leg just now. Any of you hombres reckon you can get me to the doc's?"

"Well, now that I've finally found you under all that muck, I have to say you won't be riding for several weeks, Ranger," Doctor Gibson stated as he finished his examination of Smoky's leg. "Luckily it's a clean break, but you will have to be in a cast." After the mud fight, Smoky had been lifted onto Jim Huggins' horse and taken to the Fort Griffin post hospital. Doctor Gibson had been rather surprised, to put it mildly, to see the lawmen in his office yet again. Blawcyzk and Flores had remained with Smoky while the newly arrived Rangers headed for the livery stable to put up their horses, then the hotel to obtain rooms for themselves. Still covered in dried mud, the two partners and Cindy Lou stood by while Gibson worked on his patient.

"Smoky, I never meant to hurt you. It's just that you made me so mad," Cindy Lou tearfully explained as she saw McCue's jaw tighten while Gibson set the broken leg.

"It's okay, Cindy," Smoky gritted against the pain. "It was my own fault for what I said to you."

"Smoky, Rudy and I have to be gettin' back to town," Jim spoke up. "I've got to go over things with Jim Huggins and the rest of the boys before I leave and I plan on ridin' out at sunup, so I want to hit the sack early. I'll let Captain Trumbull know what happened. Are you gonna be all right?"

"I'll make sure he is, Lieutenant," Cindy answered as she leaned down to plant a kiss on Smoky's mud smeared cheek.

"Yes, I guess he will be at that. You're his kind of nurse, Miss Cindy Lou," Blawcyzk grinned. "And you'd better make that Jim instead of Lieutenant," he added. "I have a feeling we'll be seeing a lot more of each other."

"Ah, just get outta here, Jim," Smoky snarled good-naturedly.

"Sure, pard," Jim smiled. "C'mon, Rudy, let's head for the barber shop to get baths and shaved. I can see we're not needed here." He shook his head in bemusement as Cindy Lou fussed over her injured man.

"Smoke, as soon as you can ride again, make sure you wire Captain Trumbull," Jim ordered. "I'll miss havin' you side me, pardner."

"Same here, Jim," Smoky replied. "Now get outta here before you make me start bawlin'." Smoky's attention was already focused on his nurse.

"All right, *Barnabas!*" Jim quickly ducked out, chuckling as a medicine bottle Smoky had grabbed and tossed at his head crashed against the slamming door.

CHAPTER 21

"Jim, I'm going to make cornbread for your breakfast tomorrow if you'd like. I know it's one of your favorites." Julia said, eyeing her husband as he leaned on the porch rail, gazing pensively across the ranch yard at the rising full moon, which loomed huge and yellow on the eastern horizon. Once he had related all that had happened during his assignment, Jim had been unusually quiet since returning from north Texas, and notwithstanding her best efforts Julia had failed to draw him out. While he had been as cheerful as ever when roughhousing with Charlie, he barely spoke to Julia. Even her attempts at lovemaking had been turned aside, Jim pleading he was still too tired and hurting from his injuries. Now, with Charlie spending the next two nights at his friend Joe's house, Julia was determined to get to the bottom of whatever was troubling her husband. "Would you like that?"

"I surely would," Jim replied with a smile. "You know I love anything you cook ... well, except carrots. Sam can have those."

"That horse of yours gets enough of my food around here that he shouldn't," Julia shot back. "And don't think he's getting any of that cornbread." While outwardly she scolded, inside she was joyful. Jim's retort was the first sign he'd shown of returning to his old self.

Julia stood alongside of him and slipped an arm across his back as she leaned her head on his shoulder. She felt his skin jump underneath his shirt as he winced at her touch.

"Jim, do you really think Smoky is going to marry that woman he met up at Fort Griffin?" she questioned.

"I sure do," Jim replied. "You should have seen them together. And if anyone can tame … Smoky McCue, it's Cindy Lou Lepore." Jim took in a deep breath as he realized how close he had come to letting Smoky's real name slip out. Before leaving Fort Griffin he had visited his partner at the post hospital one last time, and Smoky had elicited Jim's promise to never reveal his true name to anyone. "They seem to be meant for each other. I wouldn't be surprised if they've found a preacher and gotten hitched already."

"I always knew Smoky would settle down once he met the right woman," Julia stated. "I hope to meet her some day."

"I'm sure you will," Jim answered. "Smoky's not going to up and quit the Rangers just because he's married. Once his leg heals he'll be heading back to Austin. He'll bring her by, I'm sure. After all, they'll need a place to live. Maybe they could stay here while they're looking for one, if you wouldn't mind. Smoky won't be living at the Headquarters barracks anymore, count on that. And business at the Silver Star Saloon is about to plummet, bet a hat on that. The gals there are sure gonna miss ol' Smoke."

"I'd like that very much if they'd agree to stay here," Julia concurred, "With luck, they might even find a home nearby. It would be wonderful to have another woman around for company while you're away, and she'll probably appreciate someone to talk to when Smoky's away from home too. And perhaps I can give her some pointers on how to put up with a fiddlefooted Texas Ranger, who can't stay home very long before the itch to be on the trail sets in again."

"I know living with me hasn't been easy, Julia," Jim sincerely replied, "but I do love you."

"I know," Julia softly answered, as she kissed him lightly on the cheek. "But why haven't you shown me that since you got home? Something's bothering you horribly, Jim."

"I'm just tired, that's all," Jim answered. "I only need a couple more days of rest, then I'll be fine."

"There's more to it than that, and keeping whatever it is bottled up inside won't help," Julia persisted, kissing his cheek again as her fingers unconsciously fumbled with the buttons of his shirt.

"Don't!" Jim ordered, more harshly than he'd intended. He pulled back from her.

"Jim, you have to tell me what's wrong," Julia insisted. Her lower lip trembled as she fought back the tears welling in her eyes.

"I … can't," Jim mumbled.

"Jim, we've been through so much together, and we've always been honest with each other. Please, don't shut me out now," Julia pleaded.

Jim heaved a deep sigh, drawing in a deep breath before reluctantly answering, "All right. You'll have to know eventually anyway." He carefully unsnapped the buttons of his shirt, revealing the livid, still-healing scar across his chest and stomach. "This is what I didn't want you to have to see," he murmured.

Julia's eyes widened for a moment, as any person's would at sight of that injury, then she whispered, "Is that all that's been keeping you from me?"

"Isn't that enough?" Jim gruffly responded.

"Jim, I married you because you are a loving, caring person, not for your good looks," Julia explained. "And if you don't know that by now, then perhaps I did make a mistake when I fell in love with you."

"Oh, so you're saying you think I'm an ugly hombre," Jim suddenly grinned, relieved that his wife had not been repulsed by the disfiguring wound. "I guess you'd rather I slept in the barn with the horses."

"Oh, James Joseph Blawcyzk, you're impossible!" Julia retorted. "I never said that at all!"

"And you married me for my caring nature?" Jim teased. "I reckon I sure had you buffaloed."

"You keep it up and you will sleep in the barn," Julia threatened.

"I'll bet you mean that, too," Jim answered, knowing full well she didn't. Jim again grew serious for a moment as he asked, "This scar doesn't really bother you?"

"Your other scars don't, do they?" Julia answered, referring to the several old bullet and knife marks her husband's body bore. "And don't forget who doctored you back to health in Red Springs, when you arrived in town half dead from the beating you'd taken. And I've worked on far worse wounds than those when I was assisting my father with his practice. Your scars aren't all that bad."

"I guess at least they aren't as repulsive as my ugly face," Jim deadpanned.

"Jim, you … I guess I'll just have to show you how I feel about you," Julia shot back, "Like this." She ran her fingers lightly down his side, knowing Jim would be completely helpless at her touch. At their first meeting, Julia had inadvertently discovered the big, rugged Texas Ranger's main weakness. Jim was extremely ticklish along his ribs.

"Julia, stop, please! Anything but this!" Jim was convulsed with laughter, powerless as she pressed him against the porch rail.

"Am I going to hear anything ever again about that scar lessening my love for you?" Julia demanded.

"Never. I promise." Jim acquiesced.

"Are you certain?" Julia insisted.

"Absolutely," Jim promised.

"Then I'll stop," Julia agreed. As she took her hands off Jim's ribs, she added, "Jim, do you remember I promised you a swim just before you left for the Panhandle?"

"I seem to sorta remember something like that," Jim vaguely answered.

"And we never got to take that swim. It's a warm night tonight, and there's a full moon. It's the perfect evening for it." Julia replied.

"It's also a great night for fishing," Jim answered with a grin. "They'll be biting. I'll dig the worms while you get the poles."

"Jim, don't make me do this again," Julia warned, as she once again ran her fingers lightly over his ribs.

"All right, I give up," Jim yelped. "Let's go for that swim."

As they stepped from the porch and across the dusty ranch yard to begin the short walk to the swimming hole, Jim tried to apologize to his wife.

"Julia," he quietly stated, "I'm sorry I doubted you. It's just that …"

"Hush, Jim," Julia ordered. "That's enough talk. As the old saying goes, 'action speaks louder than words', cowboy."

"Then you've heard my last word on the subject, I promise," Jim softly responded, as he wrapped Julia in his arms and pressed his lips to hers.

978-0-595-44424-3
0-595-44424-5

Made in the USA
Lexington, KY
28 July 2012